$1.25

Kirra was frustrated by Matt's cynicism

"Don't you have faith that someday you'll find a woman to love?" she asked.

Matt was silent for a time. Then he answered. "You want me to be honest—no."

Kirra shivered, and he noted it with a narrowing of his eyes. "That disturbs you," he murmured.

"Yes."

He looked at her meditatively. "There are . . . attractions between men and women, friendships, but I believe all the rest is a bunch of moonshine." He paused. "Which is why a sound business proposition with a dash of the physical thrown in serves one so much better. . . ."

"Do you . . . honestly believe love doesn't exist?" Kirra whispered. "Have you never seen two people in love even after years of marriage?"

As she waited for his answer, she wondered if there was anything that would dent his casual, supremely male arrogance.

LINDSAY ARMSTRONG married an accountant from New Zealand and settled down—if you can call it that—in Australia. A coast-to-coast camping trip later, they moved to a six-hundred-acre mixed-grain property, which they eventually abandoned to the mice and leeches and black flies. Then, after a winning career at the track with an untried trotter, purchased ''mainly because he had blue eyes,'' they opted for a more conventional family life with their five children in Brisbane, where Lindsay now writes.

Books by Lindsay Armstrong

HARLEQUIN ROMANCE

2443—SPITFIRE
2497—MY DEAR INNOCENT
2582—PERHAPS LOVE
2653—DON'T CALL IT LOVE
2785—SOME SAY LOVE
2876—THE HEART OF THE MATTER
2893—WHEN THE NIGHT GROWS COLD

HARLEQUIN PRESENTS

887—LOVE ME NOT
927—AN ELUSIVE MISTRESS
951—SURRENDER MY HEART
983—STANDING ON THE OUTSIDE
1039—THE SHADOW OF MOONLIGHT
1071—RELUCTANT WIFE
1095—WHEN YOU LEAVE ME
1183—HEAT OF THE MOMENT

THE MARRYING GAME

Lindsay Armstrong

Harlequin Books

TORONTO • NEW YORK • LONDON
AMSTERDAM • PARIS • SYDNEY • HAMBURG
STOCKHOLM • ATHENS • TOKYO • MILAN

Original hardcover edition published in 1989
by Mills & Boon Limited

ISBN 0-373-03013-4

Harlequin Romance first edition November 1989

CHAPTER ONE

LOVER'S POINT jutted into the sea from between two beaches. One was long and white and stretched southward into the distance, while the other curved about a perfect little bay with a steep green cliff behind it, rising to the road. Across the road were a variety of residences, but for the most part they were shuttered holiday homes that saw their owners infrequently.

It was from a renovated building of four flats opposite the Point that Kirra Munro stepped into the bright morning. She was twenty-two, had shining dark hair that touched her shoulders, blue-grey eyes and a classically beautiful face that was rescued from being haughty by a lovely mobile mouth and a wide smile.

She was wearing a one-piece emerald-green swimming-costume beneath an open filmy-white blouse, and the costume emphasised the lines and curves of her slender figure without being unduly revealing. She carried a fluffy navy blue beach-towel in one hand, and she stood for a long moment with the other hand raised to shade her eyes as she gazed about. There was not a soul in sight, and she breathed deeply, almost as if relaxing. This lack of people was no doubt due to the fact that it wasn't school holidays—a time when the sleepy little seaside town of Yamba on the Clarence River suffered a population explosion.

And it caused Kirra to smile faintly in

appreciation as she crossed the road, took the steep, winding steps down to the bay, dropped her things on to the beach and waded into the surf.

The water was beautiful, fresh and invigorating, and the only company she had was a school of dolphin frolicking further out.

She came out regretfully after about half an hour, smoothing the wet hair off her forehead, and looked back out to sea—it stretched away towards the horizon like a swathe of pale blue rippled silk, so beautiful it hurt her heart. But then, she reflected, her heart was in a peculiar state of flux, once again. And that was why she was here, to try to read it . . .

That was when Lover's Point claimed her notice once more, and she decided to explore it.

It was a steep climb up a sand dune, but once up she could see Lover's, as the locals called it, with a bird's-eye view: a smooth grassy dome surrounded by a shelf of flat rock and broadening from the narrower ridge of sand and bush where she stood.

For several minutes she pondered whether to walk round the rocky, plate-like shelf that was alive with seagulls enjoying the outgoing tide, or straight down the middle, but the fact that she had no shoes settled the matter and she opted for the middle course, setting off with a long stride and a sense of anticipation that brought a wry look to her eyes as she wondered if this was how Cortés had felt.

But the sand and the spindly casuarinas gave way to rougher ground and thicker bush, and she faltered suddenly and sank down with a sharp exclamation of pain. Her eyes widened as she awkwardly inspected her heel and saw the jagged sliver of wood in it, for it was obvious that this was going to be no easily-dealt-with splinter. But she gritted her teeth and tried to pull it out, only to have it break between her nails just above the skin. She sighed exasperatedly and decided there was nothing for it but to limp home where she had a pair of tweezers.

But even putting the weight on the ball of her foot was painful, she found, as she limped a few steps, then sat down, biting her lip. 'Oh, damn,' she muttered, 'this is ridiculous!' And got up again determinedly—only to collapse once more, but this time more from fright than pain as the bushes parted and a tall man appeared in front of her.

'Oh!' she gasped, as the stranger stopped in surprise and lowered a basket and fishing-rod to the ground. 'You gave me such a fright!'

'So it would appear,' the man agreed, with the corners of his mouth twitching. 'Let me help you up. I'm quite harmless, you know.'

Kirra found herself smiling weakly. 'It wasn't only that—I've got a splinter in my foot that's killing me. I don't suppose you'd have a pair of tweezers on you?' she asked with an attempt at humour, since, as he was only wearing a pair of faded canvas shorts, it was highly unlikely. He was also, she noted, well built with wide shoulders and, she realised a second or so later, standing over her and looking down at her with a faint but unmistakable glint of appreciation in his eyes as he took in her long, slender legs and the green swimsuit that was moulded to her body beneath her flimsy and damp blouse.

Something in his gaze held her captive briefly, then just as she'd decided she'd had enough of it, appreciative or otherwise, and started to tilt her chin defiantly at him, he smiled at her and the corners of his eyes crinkled so attractively that she took an unexpected breath.

He said, 'Not on me, I'm afraid. But I think I might have a pair in my first-aid kit. Let's have a look.'

He knelt down beside her and picked up her foot, and Kirra felt her flesh prickle with a strange awareness as she studied the long, strong lines of his tanned back which was turned towards her. She licked her lips. 'Can you see it?'

'Mm. Can you walk or should I carry you?' He put her foot down gently.

She grimaced. 'I'm not exactly a lightweight. Perhaps if I could use you as a crutch . . . Would you mind?'

'Not at all,' he said easily, and just as easily slid his arms beneath her and stood up in a fluid, unhurried movement.

Kirra opened her mouth to protest, but he looked down at her with so much laughter in his hazel eyes that she found herself quite unexpectedly smiling back at him like a trusting child. But she did say, 'What about your things?'

'I'll come back for them.' He shouldered the bushes aside and she turned her face towards his body to escape the leafy twigs—and experienced a peculiar desire to rub her cheek against his smooth brown skin. Really, Kirra! she thought with an inward grin, and lifted her head immediately, only to tense visibly.

'What is it?'

'You're going the wrong way—the road's back there.'

'If,' he said, glancing down into her wary blue-grey eyes, 'you're worried that I'm about to kidnap you or anything else unpleasant, you needn't be.'

Kirra felt her face flame. 'I . . . what I mean is . . .' She trailed off lamely.

'I know what you mean,' he said, and she could tell that he was laughing at her again inwardly, but just as she stiffened resentfully he added, 'I'm camped on the Point, you see. And,' he lowered her to the ground but kept his arm around her, 'here we are.'

Kirra stood on one foot and looked around. They were in a small hollow with thick turf beneath their feet, and in front of them was a khaki tent with a blue awning, pitched beneath a clump of ti-trees. Behind them, she saw as she turned awkwardly, the ground fell away sharply so that from the tent there would be a fabulous view of sea and surf and the coastline stretching into the distance.

'Oh!' she exclaimed, then, 'What a marvellous idea! Have you been here long?'

'A few days. Why don't you sit down?' He helped her to a canvas chair beneath the awning. Then he searched through a knapsack and produced a tin with a red cross on it. 'I've never had to use this before, so I'm not sure . . . ah, yes, tweezers, some antiseptic and Band-Aids.' He looked up at her and said with a lurking grin, 'All we need is a bullet for you to bite.'

She giggled. 'How about a slug of bourbon without the branchwater?'

'Uh . . . Scotch? For medicinal purposes, of course,' he offered gravely.

'No, thanks,' she laughed. 'I'll just rely on my

stiff upper lip. I'm quite good at that, I'm told.'

But a few minutes later she wasn't so sure of it. The splinter was out and revealed as a good inch long with a wickedly sharp point, and her eyes were shimmering with tears.

She swallowed and sniffed as she looked at it lying in the palm of his hand, and then wiped her nose with the back of her hand. 'Sorry. I'm not usually such a baby.'

'I thought you were rather brave,' he said quietly as he poured antiseptic on to her heel and then stuck on a Band Aid. 'There. How about that Scotch now?'

She nodded, and he produced a bottle and poured a couple of stiffish tots into two tin mugs and handed her one. She took a sip and felt the warmth of it course through her body and sighed. Then she looked up at him with a grin and raised her mug. 'Here's to a Good Samaritan. I'm sorry I cherished some unkind thoughts about you.'

He raised his eyebrows quizzically. 'You weren't to know. Would you like to stay for lunch—as we've sorted that out?'

She looked at him questioningly.

'I've got four freshly caught bream in my basket and some damper I made this morning. How does that sound?'

'It sounds—magical,' she said slowly.

'Right! Stay where you are, ma'am. Lunch will be ready in a tick.'

Kirra sat in the filtered sunlight, nursing her mug and grappling with a feeling of mingled delight and unreality as she watched her rescuer prepare the meal. He had retrieved his fishing gear and her towel and lit a small primus, and in no time at all the bream were sizzling aromatically in a pan.

'I hope I bump into you the next time I get a splinter in my foot,' she said teasingly as she watched him take some cheese from a cool-box and grate it with a sharp knife.

He shrugged. 'I hope you never get another one like that one.'

'Are you a . . . professional wanderer?' she asked with her head to one side.

He turned the bream before answering, and sprinkled the cheese over them. Then he glinted her a green-flecked glance as he said, 'Often. Why do you ask?'

'Well, you seem so competent! As if it's home from home.'

'Have you never been camping?'

'Once.' She pulled a face. 'My mother managed to turn it into a cross between a luxury safari gone wrong and an exercise in refined torture. I had no idea it could be so simple.' She looked around. Inside the tent there was the minimum of equipment: a sleeping-bag and mattress, a pillow and a pile of books, and one small bag of clothes. Under the awning, apart from the camp table and the chair she sat in, there was only a bowl with some cooking-utensils, the cool-box and a hurricane lamp. She shook her head. 'We were so bogged down with equipment, it was unbelievable.'

He looked amused and she fell silent, wondering about his face. Not the face of a professional wanderer, she thought, or at least her conception of one, which was bearded and shaggy. This face was anything but, she decided; in fact it was rather . . . how to describe it? It gave you the impression that its owner was a sophisticated, self-contained

and very adult man. The kind of face you normally
saw above a sober suit and bent on the pursuit of
wealth or its near neighbour, power. Or both. But
his body was another matter, a thing of smooth,
powerful, streamlined elegance, and for a crazy
moment she felt a surge of something like joy at a
man who looked as if he had proved himself to
himself and didn't need to go on proving it to the
rest of the world; he wasn't yet another sleek,
pampered, faintly over-fed denizen of the world
she normally occupied, but a man simply content
to wander . . .

'What is it?'

His words brought her out of her reverie with a
start, and a faint tinge of colour to her cheeks as
she realised he was looking at her curiously.

'Nothing,' she said hastily. 'We haven't even
introduced ourselves. My name is Kirra, which is a
contraction of Kirralee. My mother maintains it's
Aboriginal—the Kirra part—but she might be
guessing.'

'Kirra . . . It fits, somehow.'

'Does it? An odd name for an odd person?'

'I didn't say that.' He laid out two plates and slid
the fish on to them. 'Is that how you see it?'

She grinned. 'No. Although there might be some
who do. Actually, I'm rather proud of it. I just
wish my mother hadn't added to it. What's yours?'

'Matthew. Commonly known as Matt—nothing
as romantic as yours.'

'Very bibical,' she said as she took a mouthful of
fish. 'Mm! This is marvellous.'

'I'm glad you approve, Kirra.'

They ate in silence for a while. Then she said
between mouthfuls, 'Where will you go from

here? Or don't you have any preconceived plans—just where the whim takes you? Or maybe you follow the fishing,' she said dreamily.

'You sound as if you'd like to do that yourself.'

'I really think I would. You might have converted me. How beautifully simple,' she said a shade drily.

'Or might you be contemplating running away from something?' he queried.

Kirra removed a bone from her mouth and looked at him, but he was eating his fish tranquilly, sitting cross-legged on the ground.

'Why do you say that?'

'You sounded—disillusioned.'

She put her knife and fork down carefully, and said slowly, 'Perhaps I am. I also feel . . . sort of hemmed in. I came away to sort it all out, actually, but . . . when you don't seem to understand yourself, that's not terribly easy, is it? Do you ever get that feeling?'

It took him so long to reply, she began to feel slightly uncomfortable, and she pictured him wondering if she wasn't as odd as her name.

Then he laughed and his eyes crinkled in that heart-stoppingly attractive way as he said, 'Don't look so worried, it's a very human way to feel. Is it on account of some man?'

Kirra hesitated. 'It's on account of me,' she said quietly, then added, 'Why do men always assume they're so bothersome to women?'

He shrugged. 'I don't know. They say it makes the world go round.'

Not mine, it doesn't, she thought. That's the problem. Then she sighed and patted her stomach appreciatively as she pushed her empty plate away.

'Do you mind if we don't talk about me any more? It's a very boring subject and not worthy of a simply splendid meal.'

'All right. What would you like to talk about?'

'Let's see . . . If I hadn't gatecrashed your camp, how would you have spent the rest of this beautiful day? More fishing?'

'Later, yes. But now I'd spend a couple of hours quite lazily, maybe reading. Then I'd go down for a swim and perhaps a spot of snorkelling off the rocks in search of crabs for dinner. And then after dinner,' he shrugged, 'listen to some music by starlight, read some more, sleep.'

Kirra stared at him with her lips parted.

'Perhaps you'd care to join me,' he said.

'Would . . . would I spoil it?'

He looked at her thoughtfully. 'You might enhance it . . .'

'I mean,' she broke in, 'I know what it's like when you really want to be alone—strangely enough that's what I thought *I* needed today, but now . . .' She broke off, flinching.

But he said simply, 'Then don't be.'

'Tell me all the places you've been to,' said Kirra.

They were sitting in front of a fire with a canopy of stars above them and the sound of the ocean all around. Out to sea there were a myriad little lights pricking the darkness as the fishing fleet from Yamba and Iluka—its twin town across the mouth of the river—trawled.

Kirra wore an old jumper many sizes too big for her over her swimsuit, and her hair was a tangle as only a head of hair that hasn't seen a comb since two swims and a sea breeze can be. But in the firelight her face glowed, as if the memory of the day that stretched behind was something precious.

As indeed it was. They had swum together and talked about everything under the sun but themselves. Then he'd shown her the rudiments of snorkelling, and she'd been enchanted, and even interested in the cooking process of the three unfortunate crabs they had caught.

Dinner had been another delicious meal: crab, asparagus from a tin, potato salad from a tin, but fresh lettuce and tomatoes from the cool-box. damper again and some Camembert and biscuits to round it off. Then they had built up the fire and Matt had spread a ground-sheet out, and for a while they had played Mozart on a battery tape-recorder.

She looked across at him as he lay stretched out and propped up on one elbow, sipping his coffee, and waited for his answer. She had learnt during the day that he often took his time before speaking—in fact, she'd learnt quite a bit about him, but perhaps most importantly that, even on a much longer acquaintance, she still mightn't know him very well. For there was a quality of detachment about him that let you in so far and no further. And there was often a glimmer of amusement in his hazel eyes as they rested on her, which should have irritated her but oddly didn't. For the rest, she knew from his conversation and speech that he was well educated, he'd told her that he was thirty-seven, admittedly in response to her asking; then he had guessed her age accurately. He had also told her that he'd travelled overseas, and that he'd grown up in Victoria.

He said at last, 'Places like this, or cities?'

'Like this, perhaps even wilder,' she said. 'I can't imagine you enjoying cities.'

He looked across at her quizzically. 'You'd be bored stiff with the wilds before very long, Kirra.'

She sighed and swirled the coffee in her mug. 'I suppose so. It's a question of being able to do without people, isn't it? How do you manage it? Was it a long hard road before . . . this happened?'

'Why do you assume I can do without people?'

'I don't know,' she mused. 'Something about you. And you did say you were a wanderer. That doesn't sound like someone who needs people too much.'

He was silent, staring into the fire. Then he said, 'You're not quite right. I do need . . . people.'

'Do you mean women?'

His hazel eyes lifted to hers. 'From time to time.'

'But that . . that's a physical need, isn't it?' she said rather drily. 'Not a mental one.'

'It all depends,' he said, watching her. 'If it's a two-way thing, then it has to be more than a physical need. Hasn't it ever happened that way for you?'

'It . . .' She broke off and bit her lip then lifted her shoulders in a curiously wry gesture and smiled faintly. 'I'm probably a bit muddled up on the subject,' she murmured, and fell silent.

'But not . . . completely inexperienced?'

Kirra looked away, then back at him. 'No.'

He held her gaze steadily until she lowered her lashes over the blue-grey of her eyes, then all he said, finally, was, 'Would you like some more coffee?'

Something that could have been a sigh of relief caught at her throat, and she nodded mutely and handed him her mug. But she couldn't help watching him as he bent over the fire to get the coffee-pot. He too wore an old jumper over his shorts, and his thick, fairish hair was ruffled and streaked with salt. And, in a flash of awareness that took her breath away and made her flesh tingle right up to the roots of her hair, she realised that she was more physically aware of this man than she had ever been in her life, and that it had been growing all day like a secret longing—that it was totally inexplicable and incredibly embarrassing, particularly in the light of her earlier words.

Then she realised he was standing in front of her, offering her her mug back, and she took it with suddenly clumsy, shaking hands and set it on the ground, but not before she had spilt some and scalded her fingers.

'I . . . I . . . after this,' she said disjointedly and hurriedly, 'I really ought to be going. It must be quite late.' She didn't dare lift her eyes, she thought with a miserable bump of her heart, because he would quite possibly be amused again.

But his voice was quiet and sober as he said, 'Why don't you stay, Kirra?'

Shock held her rigid for a moment. Then she spoke hoarsely and without thinking, 'What . . . why?'

'I thought you knew. I thought I might be having the same effect on you . . . as you're having on me.'

Her lashes flew up. 'I am. Am I?' she said shakily. 'I didn't know . . .' She stopped and licked her lips.

'Yes, you are,' he said very quietly, and held down a hand.

She took it slowly and let him draw her to her feet.

'How did you know?' she whispered, then flushed brilliantly. 'I didn't . . . was I that transparent?' She looked away.

'Does it matter?' He linked his fingers about her

wrist and, with his other hand on her chin, turned her face back towards him. 'Do you have to hide it?'

Their eyes locked. 'You managed to hide it,' she murmured.

'Mainly because I didn't want to scare the living daylights out of you. If you recall, you did wonder about me.'

'I know,' she said dazedly.

'And now?' he queried, his hazel eyes direct and almost sombre.

'Now?' she repeated, her lashes fluttering in confusion. 'Can it happen like this? So . . . like this? I feel as if I'm dreaming.'

'It can happen any way you like, Kirra.' His fingers left her chin and traced the outline of her mouth, and his eyes were suddenly curiously intent.

'What,' she caught her breath, 'do you mean? I don't . . . I don't understand . . .'

'I mean you can tell me to stop and I will. Or you could—*we* could talk about it, and how it's been for you—not exactly a picnic, I gather. Or,' his hazel gaze roamed her face, 'we could dispense with words altogether. It's up to you.' He dropped his hand and just stood there, watching her.

Kirra trembled from head to toe, and her hands came up involuntarily; she clasped them together and started to say something, but stopped, and entirely of her own free will, she was to remember for ever after, moved into his arms.

It was a long, slow kiss like no other she had known. And a communion of two bodies that moulded them to each other and left her rejoicing in the unmistakable knowledge that he did indeed want her. It was the feel of his strong hands on her body, but also the feeling that no hands had been or could be wiser or know her so well. It was the taste of him, and the way she felt at the same time languorous, with skin so silken and soft, yet electrically alive, her pulses beating an erotic tattoo that brought a faint dew of sweat to her brow as their bodies entwined and they kissed. They broke off and breathed together, then kissed again with a mutual hunger and curious urgency.

When it ended, she clasped her hands around the back of his neck and stared gravely up into his eyes. And in an unconscious gesture she loosened her interlocked fingers so that she could fiddle with the ring that was normally on her left hand . . .

It was like being shot, she remembered later. She unwound her arms and whispered distractedly, with every vestige of colour draining from her face, 'What am I doing? I must be mad . . . oh, please let me go!'

He looked down at her steadily for what seemed like an age, his eyes narrowing sardonically.

'You don't under . . . understand,' she stammered. 'I'm engaged to be married. All the arrangements are being made.' She flinched as he smiled incredulously. 'Oh, I don't know what you must think of me!'

He released her and stepped backwards. 'I think perhaps we ought to have talked first, after all,' he said coolly. 'But you still can if you'd like to.'

She put a hand to her mouth and discovered tears on her cheeks. And the enormity of what she'd done, together with the enormity of trying to explain, washed over like a black tide of despair and she whirled about and started to run.

She wasn't sure when she first became aware that he was following her. Perhaps when the blackness in front became less dense and she stopped twisting and dodging to wonder why, and turned to see the bobbing light of a torch behind her. She swallowed and gasped for air, and realised she'd lost all sense of direction and had no idea which way to go.

Then it was too late. He called her name sharply and the torchlight played over her. She stood as still as a statue as he approached, wondering fearfully what he intended to do. He was entitled to be angry, if nothing else . . .

And it was certainly anger she saw darkening his eyes as he stopped right in front of her and said coldly, 'You're mad!'

'I kn-know,' she said huskily, 'but please don't . . .'

'Don't what?' he retorted contemptuously. 'Take by force what you were so eager to offer until you changed your mind? At the moment I couldn't think of anything I'd like to do less, sweetheart,' he said deliberately, 'so set your mind at rest.' And he looked her up and down so coolly and mockingly that she flushed and set her teeth.

'Then why follow me?'

'Because you're liable to break your neck, which I couldn't fix as easily as I did the splinter. And for some perverse reason,' he smiled derisively at her, 'it amuses me not to let that happen. I feel I owe it to your fiancé,' he said with soft, cutting mockery.

Kirra closed her eyes and swallowed several times. Then she said quietly, 'All right. If you could take me to the road . . . I am lost.'

It was a strange, silent journey, and she breathed exasperatedly when she realised that she hadn't in fact been that far from the road when he had caught up with her. She said abruptly, 'Thank you. I can manage from here.'

He shone the torch about and let it linger on a

battered Land Rover parked on the verge. 'That's mine,' he said equally abruptly. 'If you've much further to go, don't be herioc about it. You never know who you might encounter at this time of night—some man not as understanding as I am, perhaps.'

She stifled the sob that rose to her throat, and gestured across the road. 'It's just over there, honestly.'

He looked at her searchingly, then shrugged and turned away. 'Goodbye, then. It's been—interesting.'

She wilted miserably beneath the scorn and derision in his voice. 'I'm *sorry*,' She said desperately. 'I . . .' She broke off and shivered, wrapping her arms about her. 'I . . . oh!' she looked down at herself. 'I'm still wearing your jumper,' she said lamely. 'Here . . .'

He turned back briefly. 'Keep it.'

She hesitated, her lips framed to say his name pleadingly, but he walked away from her to be swallowed up in the darkness, so that all she could see was the light of the torch. She watched until she couldn't see even that. Then she turned wearily and walked home.

But she didn't fall asleep until the early hours of the morning, and then it was a restless, tormented slumber invaded by a peculiar sense of doom. When she finally dragged herself from it, it was to stumble straight out on to the balcony and immediately have that subconscious prediction of doom fulfilled. For the Land Rover was gone.

CHAPTER TWO

Six weeks later Kirra ran the last few steps to her front door, fumbling desperately for her key, and burst inside to the shrilling telephone.

'Hello?' she said breathlessly.

'Kirralee? Is that you, dear?'

'Yes, Mum,' Kirra replied with patient affection. 'I've just got home. I heard the phone ringing from the passageway, that's why I took so long to answer.'

'I'd probably have tried once again. Had a busy day?'

Kirra grimaced. 'A fiddly day. What are you and Dad doing this evening?'

'We're having a dinner party.'

Kirra eased her bag off her shoulder and removed her earrings. 'Oh?'

'Yes, a business associate of your father's,' her mother said brightly. 'Someone rather interesting. We'd love you to come—that's why I'm ringing,' she added.

Kirra glanced at her watch, 'Mum,' she said reluctantly, 'it's a bit late, and I don't really feel like socialising.'

'Darling,' Naomi Munro said with concern, 'since you came home from that mystery trip to New South Wales, you've been in a rather strange mood altogether. Is something wrong? Something you'd like to tell me? I won't press you but . . .' She broke off, then said in a rush, 'Postponing the wedding, for example—not that I would want you to get married unless you were absolutely sure, but . . .' She paused again. 'Has Jeremy . . .'

'It's nothing to do with Jeremy,' Kirra broke in. 'It's . . . me. I just feel—I don't know how to describe it—*restless*,' she said on a curious note of bitterness.

'Has something happened to make you feel this way?' her mother queried.

Yes, Kirra thought. If only I could forget . . . She said wearily, 'Not really, and wondered why she couldn't confide in her mother. Probably something to do with having gone against her parents' advice once, and having reaped the consequences.

'Well, then, you've done the right thing,' Naomi said soothingly, although she added wryly, 'It's fortunate Jeremy is so patient.'

'When you're marrying the heir to the Munro fortune you can afford to be—or to put it another way, you can't afford not to be patient,' Kirra said with an unmistakable note of strain and cynicism in her voice.

Her mother was silent for an unusually long time. Then she said, more confusedly than reproachfully, Kirra thought absently, 'Darling, Jeremy isn't like that, is he?'

Kirra closed her eyes. 'No. No, he's not. I shouldn't have said that. Mum . . .'

'Kirra, why don't you come to dinner tonight? It will be a change from brooding, at least.'

'I . . . all right,' Kirra said with a sigh.

It was just before seven-thirty when she parked her little sports car beneath the portico of the fabulous house she had always thought of as home. Situated on a bend of the Nerang River, it was a minor mansion in large grounds, and she sat for a moment staring absently ahead, then stepped out of the car and shook out her skirt.

Her dress was lavender-blue, with a finely pleated, strapless bodice and a clinging skirt that nevertheless had yards of filmy material in it. From the bodice her shoulders rose smooth and gleaming and quite unadorned. In fact, the only jewellery she wore was her diamond engagement ring and a fine gold chain on her wrist. Her hair was parted in the middle, showing a perfect widow's peak and cascading to her shoulders, dark and gleaming. She'd taken a few extra minutes to make her face up with care, and the result was glamourous but understated.

Stanley greeted her at the front door as he greeted everyone, and her face softened. Stanley was a permanent fixture in the Munro household. Both he and her father had been career soldiers, and had known each other from not long after her father had graduated from the Royal Military College in Duntroon. But whereas Kenneth Munro had risen to the rank of Major-General and been knighted, Stanley had been content to be his batman.

When Sir Kenneth had retired from the army to concentrate his time on his family and his business, Stanley had moved into the household and assumed a variety of roles: butler and chauffeur to name a couple. It was impossible to imagine the family without Stanley now.

And he greeted Kirra warmly and told her her parents were waiting for her in the living-room.

It was a magnificent room with cream carpeting, cream damask settees, soft green occasional chairs with fine, carved frames and spindly legs, paintings and exquisite lamps, and on the settees, cushions of every hydrangea blue and pink. A room to make you catch your breath, which Kirra did, but for a different reason, as she paused on the threshold and caught sight of her parents standing on the terrace just beyond, with their arms linked and her mother resting her head on her father's shoulder.

And she felt her heart contract at the sight of the two people she loved most in the world, two people who, although rather older than average parents, had brought her up with such care and so much love. Her gentle, scholarly father who was possibly the least likely-looking Major-General, but certainly had a passion for translating Caesar's Gallic wars, her bright, sometimes irrespressible mother . . . How come I get so mixed up, she thought bleakly, make such mistakes after all they've done for me?

Then her mother turned and saw her, and her eyes lit up warmly as they always did, but Kirra noticed, as she went forward to kiss them, that her father looked tired.

'Dad,' she said anxiously, what have you been doing? You look . . .'

'Old?' her father queried with a grin. 'I am getting on, you know, pet. Like a sherry?'

'Thanks, but I didn't mean . . .' Kirra broke off and accepted a glass from her father. Then the doorbell chimed musically and she realised she had no idea who her parents were entertaining. 'By the way, who . . .'

But Stanley appeared in the doorway and murmured, 'Mr Remington, sir.' He moved aside and a tall, fair man walked into the room. At the same time, Kirra choked on her sherry . . .

It *can't* be, she thought incredulously as she

coughed and turned away, and her mother hovered
anxiously, ready to bang her on the back. Oh, God!

'No, I'm all right,' she muttered to her mother
and, with the greatest reluctance, turned back to see
her father with his hand outstretched to greet his
guest, but looking back at her. As for Matthew
Remington, he was looking at her with the beginning
of a faint smile on his lips, and a look of sardonic
amusement creeping into his eyes.

Then it was wiped out as her father turned back to
him and said in his old-fashioned, courteous manner,
'Welcome to our home, Matt. May I introduce you
to my wife, Naomi . . . and our daughter, Kirra—she
doesn't make a practice of greeting guests this way, I
can assure you,' he added with a mischievous smile.
'All right now love?' he asked Kirra.

'I'm fine,' Kirra murmured, but she found that the
muscles of her throat felt stiff. She extended her hand
as her mother had done, but couldn't bring herself to
look up as she said, 'How do you do?' Here it comes!
she thought. He's going to say . . . we've already met,
or, she fell down by way of greeting me last time
or . . . I've had some experience of your daughter, Sir
Kenneth.

Matt Remington echoed none of her fevered
imaginings, but he did keep hold of her hand until
she was forced to look up, and then he said, 'What
an unusual name. How do you do, Kirra?'

And while part of her sighed with relief, another
part of her found itself screwed up into a tangle of
emotions that defied description, although bitter
resentment was certainly one of them as those hazel
eyes rested on her face with that hateful amusement
back again.

'It is, isn't it?' her mother said brightly. 'Actually,

it's Kirralee, but I'm the only one who doesn't shorten it. For years I thought it was an Aboriginal word, but I've never been able to find out what it means.'

'Really?' Matt said, as if he'd not heard any of this before.

'Yes, really.' Naomi smiled ruefully and put her arm through his in her own peculiarly natural way. 'Come, let us get you a drink.'

Kirra watched as they walked away, his fair head bent attentively towards her mother, and closed her eyes.

'That was a truly delicious dinner, Lady Munro,' Matt Remington said. They were back in the living-room with their coffee, and Kirra's father was pouring liqueurs.

No, it wasn't, Kirra thought darkly as she fiddled absently with her engagement ring and listened with half an ear to the conversation. It tasted like sawdust to me, and I can't believe this isn't some ghastly nightmare. A professional wanderer, eh?

She glanced through her lashes towards the settee her mother shared with their guest. He looked so perfectly at home. As if his black dinner-suit had been made for him, which it probably had; and with his snowy-white shirt front perfectly laundered and his thick fair hair smooth and tamed . . . He looked as if he could be anything, a successful politician, a mining magnate, she pondered, anything but a professional wanderer content to roam far and wide away from the bright lights and the dollar signs. Oh, Kirra, what a fool you made of yourself and let him make of you! And to *think* that for the past six weeks you've been perfectly miserable and actually wondered if you shouldn't have thrown up everything and thrown your lot in with his for a week or a year or however long he wanted you . . .

She came out of her painful musings with a start, to see her mother looking at her strangely.

'I'm sorry, I was dreaming,' she said quietly.

'I was just telling Matt about Jeremy.'

Kirra squirmed inwardly, but managed to meet that cool hazel gaze calmly.

'You have my best wishes,' he murmured, and if there was a hint of derision in his voice, only Kirra seemed to notice it.

'Thank you.'

'When is the big day?'

Her mother rushed in before Kirra could speak, 'She hasn't quite made up her mind.'

'Oh?' he smiled at Kirra with his eyebrows raised quizzically and his head turned away from Naomi Munro; and there was so much insolence in his smile, Kirra bit her lip and curbed a desire to rise swiftly and slap his face. Then he added, 'Well, that is the lady's prerogative, I believe.'

'Don't you encourage her!' Naomi said playfully. 'Tell me, are you married?'

'No.'

'Now that surprises me,' Kirra's mother said with the forthrightness for which she was famed. 'That you've managed to elude it, I mean, ' she added with a twinkle in her eyes. 'I would have thought the girls would have been queuing for the honour—and I'm renowned for my judgement in these matters, aren't I, Kenneth?'

'I suppose that's why you chose me,' Sir Kenneth teased.

'Of course! Nothing but the best.'

Kirra moved restlessly in her chair, but Matt Remington laughed and the conversation proceeded easily, although to those who knew her she herself was unusually quiet. He kept up the game of pretending not to know her superbly, however, apart from the odd glance which spoke volumes to her, and he showed no sign of being put out by her silences, which for the life of her she couldn't help. In fact he was the perfect guest, interested in her father's military background, knowledgeable about Renaissance art which was her mother's ruling passion.

It did strike Kirra a little odd once that, for business associates, there was no business discussed except in the most general terms, but then her father held to the old-fashioned view that one did not discuss such things in front of ladies—often to his wife and daughter's exasperation.

But the *coup de grâce*, to Kirra's mind, came when Matt Remington finally took his leave. He took her hand and for a bare moment let his gaze wander over her from head to toe, as if he was mentally stripping her naked, and rejecting what he saw.

'I don't understand,' Kirra said tautly to her mother while her father saw Matt Remington to his car. 'Who is he?'

'A very wealthy man,' Naomi Munro replied thoughtfully, and sighed uncharacteristically.

'So?' Kirra hoped the sardonic note with which the word came out was lost on her mother, but it was a vain hope.

Naomi sank down into a chair. 'You didn't like him. I find that rather strange.'

'Does it matter? I . . .' Kirra moved abruptly,

'I think I should have stayed home,' she said re-gretfully then. 'I didn't mean to be rude to your guest. Perhaps if I'd known more about him . . .' she added ruefully as she sat down herself.

'About Matt Remington?' her father queried, coming back into the room. 'What would you like to know?'

'Well,' Kirra said helplessly, 'what kind of a business associate, how long you've known him, why . . .' She stopped.

'He heads quite a large group of companies, at least one of which is closely related to our business. I haven't known him for long, although of course most people have heard of him, not only for his meteoric rise to fame but because of his father, but I must say I liked him', her father said with a strained smile.

Kirra opened her mouth to say that *she* had never heard the name before, but something in the way her father turned away from her gave her the impression he didn't want to talk about it any more, and she hesitated, then said instead, 'Dad, I'm sorry . . .'

'That's all right, my dear; We all have our off nights.' He turned back and looked at her rather penetratingly though, then added, with a deliberate effort at brightness she thought, 'How about a nightcap, girls? You drank very sparingly tonight, Kirra. I think you could afford a small one before you go, and you look as if you could do with it.'

Kirra drove home feeling guilty and totally at odds with herself, not to mention angry and confused.

Angry not only with Matt Remington and his insolent looks, but with fate, which had seen fit to cast up her monumental indiscretion at her like this, and fate again for allowing her to be one of the few people who had never heard of Matthew Remington—or his father, for that matter.

She nosed her car into the underground parking-garage of her apartment block which was across the road from Main Beach, switched off and leant her head wearily against the back of the seat. I suppose, she mused, the best thing to do is forget about it—what's been done can't be undone. Forget? she said to herself mockingly then. Aren't you forgetting the fact that you've thought of him pretty constantly for these past six weeks, or do you think that because you've discovered he also deceived you, it will make a difference?

'Why shouldn't it?' she murmured aloud. 'I didn't *deliberately* set out to deceive him either.' She broke off and felt the familiar colour rise to her cheeks as she thought yet again of her incredible lapse on Lover's Point. Then she set her teeth and tried to conjure up a picture of Jeremy in her mind's eye.

Jeremy, who was as tall as Matt Remington but with a ganglier frame; Jeremy, with his bespectacled grey eyes that glowed so engagingly when he talked about his life's work—he was a research chemist—and who loved her steadily, if undramatically, something she found so reasurring after Bret.

But all she could come up with was a pair of cool, mocking, hazel eyes and, to her horror, a quicker pulse-rate and a peculiar sensation at the pit of her stomach—signs she recognised all too well, and she flinched and got out of the car swiftly and slammed the door.

The next day she had lunch with her friend Philippa West, commonly know as Pippa. They had been to school together and Philippa was now married to an architect who sometimes worked in close association with the interior decorating firm Kirra worked for.

And after the usual chitchat and making enquiries about the house Pippa and Marcus were building, Kirra heard herself say, 'Pip, have you ever heard of Matthew Remington?'

Pippa narrowed her eyes thoughtfully. 'Who hasn't?'

Kirra grimaced. 'Me. I believe he has a famous father, too.'

'Yes—Jack Remington. He was a racing driver and playboy *par excellence*. He also ran through the family fortune several times over and was jolly lucky he had a son able to recoup them—particularly after he ran away with and married his girlfriend.'

Kirra blinked several times. 'Come again?'

Pippa smiled. 'Where've you been all these years?'

'I can't imagine,' Kirra said honestly. 'I loathe and detest motor-racing, so perhaps that's why I missed it all.'

'Well,' Pippa settled herself more comfortably, 'as the wife of a car fanatic, you've come to the right person. Apparently Jack Remington looked with scorn on his family's solid business background, and set out upon inheriting it, he was the only child, to blow it on fast cars and fast women, despite the fact he had a wife. The—er—product of that union is said son Matthew, and it was after his mother died that his father became enamoured of Matt's girlfriend. Fortunately, Jack didn't quite inherit all that the Remingtons over the years had so industriously achieved. He had a maiden aunt who had the foresight to bypass him and leave her share of it to his son. Word hath it that Matt Remington has increased that small inheritance tenfold by ten, is now a wealthier man than his father ever was and is able to cock his snoot at him . . . and his ex-girlfriend, who is now his stepmother—darling, you'll catch a fly in a minute,' Pippa said gently. And as Kirra shut her mouth with a click, she asked, 'Tell me why all this should be so riveting.'

'I . . . I met him recently,' Kirra said uncomfortably. 'That's all.'

Pippa smiled slightly. 'I believe—despite their differences in other respects, father and son have one thing in common—a devastating effect on women.'

'I wouldn't know about that,' Kirra said, with a total disregard for the truth but an overriding instinct for self-preservation, she later realised. 'So . . . he's a lover and a leaver, is he?'

Pippa shrugged. 'There've been a lot of women, by all accounts. No one's trapped him as yet, though. How did you come to meet him?'

'Through my parents,' Kirra said slowly.

Pippa finished her coffee and dabbled her mouth. 'How's Jeremy?' she asked, shooting Kirra a rather keen look.

'Fine!'

'Good,' Pippa murmured, and looked as if she had been going to say something but changed her mind at the last minute. 'You will both come to the house-warming, won't you? I can't give an exact date yet, but it should only be about six weeks away—that's if Marcus doesn't change his mind and decide to pull it all down and start again.'

Kirra laughed. 'He wouldn't!'

'Honestly, my dear,' Pippa said ruefully, 'he's *obsessed* with getting this house *perfect*!'

'I bet it will be, too,' Kirra said warmly, and

glanced at her watch. 'Time I was getting back to work. I'm afraid.' She pulled a face.

Pippa raised an eyebrow. 'Thought you loved your job?'

'I do,' Kirra said hastily. 'I do.'

But when she was back doing her beloved job, she had to acknowledge she was feeling restless even at work which really alarmed her because she did love her job. 'Damn him,' she muttered, but stopped to think of what she'd just learnt about Matthew Remington, which altered the picture yet again and undeniably in her favour, she thought. At least I didn't join a long line of discarded lovers, and they certainly sound like a family to stay away from—I wonder if it's all true. Pippa's not given to passing on idle gossip, but it sounds . . . it just sounds too bizarre to be true. Anyway, it's none of my business now, thank God, and perhaps knowing about all the women in his past will help me to forget.

The days passed with not a great deal of change to her state of mind, however—and there was Jeremy in the flesh, not just a mental picture so oddly hard to conjure up.

She cooked him dinner one evening and arranged to spend the following Sunday with him. Their evening was spent quietly together and he made no mention of the postponed wedding plans. But he kissed her goodnight with unusual fervour, and she found herself incredibly touched and almost prepared to think of a wedding date again. She also found herself trying to analyse their relationship.

She felt safe with Jeremy, she realised, which was important to her. He knew about the hectic times with Bret and how much she had been hurt. He understood, although this sometimes niggled her curiously, why she mistrusted a physical relationship, and he was content to wait until they were married for that. Perhaps, she thought with a sudden flash of acuteness, she imagined this was how her father would have conducted his courtship of her mother, and their marriage had certainly endured. Actually—her flash of perception continued—there were some things about Jeremy that reminded her very much of her father: his temperament, a quality of uprightness that had been notably lacking in Bret and those mad halcyon days of *their* engagement.

So why did she sometimes get this niggle of doubt? That it might be a grave risk marrying a man you hadn't slept with? This was the way it was supposed to be done, and if anyone should know how one's body could betray one, she should.

And then there was Jeremy's quiet conviction that he loved her.

I must have been mad, she mused. What did get into me? Perhaps all prospective brides suffered moments of panic, and Matt Remington represented something free and unrestrained, unsigned and unsealed. Yes . . . that was part of the attraction.

She shivered suddenly and deliberately turned her thoughts back to Jeremy.

Sunday was hot and sultry, and they teamed up with some friends in the afternoon to go to a charity rodeo at Nerang. Then, when Jeremy was going to drop her home and go on to have a game of squash, she said impulsively, 'Drop me off at Mum and Dad's instead. I think a swim in their pool is the only sane thing to do in this heat. The beach will be too windy.'

Jeremy changed direction cheerfully.

'Sure you wouldn't like to do that yourself?' she asked. 'I can guarantee they'll give us something long and cool to drink and they'll probably feed us.'

Jeremy grinned. 'That sounds awfully tempting, but I promised this bloke a game and I've had to put it off a couple of times already. Besides I need the exercise.'

Kirra laughed. 'Anyone would think you were fat!'

'Prevention is the key word. It's been known to happen even to beanstalks like myself.' He looked at her gravely, but his eyes were twinkling behind his glasses.

Kirra was assailed by a sudden rush of affection. 'You're my favourite beanstalk, you know,' she said huskily.

His eyes changed and she thought he was going to say something but instead he looked back at the road and concentrated rather intently on his driving.

There was an unfamiliar blue Rolls-Royce in her parents' driveway and Kirra grimaced.

Jeremy pulled up. 'Anyone you know?'

'No. But if they're here on a Sunday, they must be fun. Mum maintains a strict rule about Sunday entertaining—it's got to be people whose company they really enjoy. Will we go to that movie on Tuesday night?' She gathered her belongings and looked at him enquiringly.

'Why not? It sounds good. I'll pick you up.' He leant over and kissed her cheek, then added quietly, 'Love you, Kirra.'

Sunday was Stanley's day off, so Kirra let herself in with her key, guessing that her parents and their guests would be at the poolside on the other side of the house. She hesitated briefly, then decided she was dusty and windblown and she might as well change into her costume first.

She still had her own bedroom and kept some spare clothes there. The costume she slipped into was a rose-pink lycra, and she brushed her hair vigorously, shaped her eyebrows absently and, armed with a fluffy white towel, sallied forth.

She was half-way down the lushly carpeted passageway that led to the pool patio and the murmur of voices beyond, when the outer screen door opened and a tall figure filled the doorway, dark and almost unrecognisable because of the glow of sunset behind.

Almost, but not quite . . .

CHAPTER THREE

'WHAT the hell are you doing here?'

The words slipped out before Kirra could stop herself, although she stopped walking as if she had been shot.

Matt Remington, however, displayed no such surprise, he too stopped, but to raise his eyebrows at her quizzically and to lounge against the doorframe comfortably. Nor did he say anything, but crossed his arms—all he wore, she noted, was a pair of navy-blue trunks—and he continued to observe her as the silence lengthened.

Kirra licked her lips, slipping from shock and spontaneous anger to a feeling of foolish embarrassment.

'I beg your pardon,' she said stiffly. 'That was—rude of me. I just didn't expect . . . you were the last person I expected to see . . .' She trailed off, hating herself for sounding so inarticulate and placating.

A slight smile twisted his lips, as if he could read her thoughts perfectly. 'Expected to see—or hoped never to see again?' he asked softly.

'Yes, well, there is that,' she conceded with a return of some spirit. But then her shoulders slumped, because it was all so impossibly awkward. She knew that within minutes her parents would discover her presence, and there was no way she would be able to get out of staying.

Matt Remington straightened then and came

towards her, right up to her so that she had to tilt her head to look up into those hazel eyes, her own eyes wide and wary.

'I guess we'll just have to make the the best of it,' he murmured, and added, 'Your . . . our secret is safe with me, by the way.'

'What secret?' That slipped out too, and she could have cried with frustration as his eyes mocked her and he drawled, 'Why your lost day with me, Kirra. The day you forgot all about—Jeremy, isn't it? Yes,' he continued barely audibly, 'and such a *nice* young man, your mother assures me. Does he know how vulnerable you are to the fleeting attractions of passing strangers?'

What Kirra would have replied was, perhaps fortunately, lost, because just as she had predicted her mother came through the screen door, stopped, blinked, then rushed into disjointed speech.

'I *thought* I heard voices—darling, I didn't know you were here—what a surprise! How . . . nice, we're going to have a cold supper round the pool and now we'll be a foursome.' She stopped, rather like a clock running down, and Kirra frowned faintly because it was unlike her mother to sound . . . *lame*, yes, that was it. Or to have a . . . pleading look in her eyes? Oh God, I must have been worse than I realised the other night, she thought, and Mum's afraid I'm going to put on another display of surliness, which in her book is unforgivable, especially on Sunday.

She took a deep breath, ignored the speculative look in her tormentor's eye—well, that was what he was—and managed to say brightly, 'I'd love to have supper with you, I'm dying for a swim and,' she paused briefly but forced herself to go on, 'perhaps I should show Mr Remington a better side of me. I must apologise for the other night.' She looked at him directly. 'I was rather—out of sorts.' Make of that what you will she thought defiantly, while somehow managing to smile at him.

He smiled right back. 'Call me Matt, Kirra.'

Her mother's sigh of relief was audible.

The pool was heavenly as the sun sank below the horizon and the first faint stars pricked the velvety blue sky.

'This is the life, eh, Matt?' her father said.

Kirra, alone in the pool, sighed regretfully and decided it was time to get out and be sociable, or at least help her mother. But it was not easy to climb out unselfconsciously beneath Matt Remington's gaze, at least what she had felt to be his gaze on her ever since she'd dived into the crystal-clear water. Yet when she had looked at him obliquely he'd been lying back in a cane lounger, studying either his glass or her father.

Why *is* he here again? she wondered. For someone I'd never heard of before, he's achieved the status of an honoured guest.

But it was true, she acknowledged, that because her father's office, and the head office of the flourishing fine condiment business which her grandfather had started and which had made Munro's a household name in Australia, was forty miles away in Brisbane it was not uncommon for him to deal with local business matters and contracts from his study at home. Quite possibly they'd been closeted there during the afternoon, and it would have been only natural for her mother to offer a refreshing swim and supper afterwards.

On a Sunday, though? But then they obviously liked Matt Remington rather a lot . . .

She bit her lip perplexedly, then shrugged. It was nothing to do with her really, just supremely inconvenient and embarrassing! But she climbed out of the pool saying brightly. 'That was marvellous! Just what I needed. I'll give Mum a hand.'

'Stay where you are, Kirralee.' Her mother's disembodied voice floated out from the direction of the kitchen window. 'It's all ready—just needs assembling.'

Kirra hesitated, then sank down into a chair and accepted a drink from her father. She brushed her sleek, wet hair back. 'So,' she said, and thought it sounded rather desperate but pressed on, 'you're . . . do you live here on the coast . . . Matt?'

A flicker of a smile crept into his eyes. 'Actually, I'm something of a nomad,' he replied politely. 'The one place I call home, I see all too infrequently, unfortunately.'

'And where is that?' Kirra asked equally politely, although thinking—you have an incredible nerve even to mention the word nomad!

'On the Tweed,' he said briefly. 'But I do have a base in Surfers' now.'

'Here we are . . .' It was her mother bearing a tray to Kirra's relief and the next two hours passed fairly pleasantly as they ate delicious cold chicken and salad followed by a cheesecake, and drank a superb Riesling.

In fact, once or twice Kirra was moved to amazement at how natural she was able to be, and was forced to conclude that Matt Remington was making it easy for her. Since their encounter in the passage and his remark about nomads there had been no further looks of veiled mockery, and it was easy to see why her parents were so taken with their new friend. Just as I was, she thought, and caught her breath as for a moment she was transported back to Lover's Point and another starlit night.

She closed her eyes briefly, unable to forget the sequel to that marvellous evening and how she'd fallen prey to . . . whatever it was she had fallen prey to. He's an . . . enigma, she mused, lifting her lashes and glancing at Matt through them. What was he doing *there*, anyway? And how could he now have her feeling almost comfortable—well, slightly less consumed by a crazy mixture of embarrassment at her behaviour and outrage that he should have duped her so?

Which he had, she reminded herself, and paused confusedly to wonder what she would have felt if she'd met him again and he'd been exactly what she had thought he was. For that matter—the old puzzle rose up to taunt her—why had it been so appealing? How much had been the man, and how much . . .

She sighed and realised everyone was looking at her with varying degrees of amusement.

'That sounded as if you have the weight of the world on your shoulders, pet,' her father said.

'No—just tired,' she answered, and added ruefully, because it had obviously made her parents happy to see her behaving so much better, 'I hope you don't think I'm being rude again, Matt, but it's work tomorrow and I think I might head off home now.' She stood up. 'Oh!'

'What?' asked Naomi.

'I forgot—Jeremy dropped me off. But no

matter, I'll ring for a taxi.'

'No need for that,' Matt Remington said, also standing up. 'I've got an early start tomorrow, so if your parents will excuse me, I could drop you off on my way home.'

Kirra opened her mouth, but her father said, 'How kind of you, Matt!'

'You didn't have to do this.'

The big blue car even smelt expensive—there seemed to be acres of cream leather in it, and it had a cabriolet top; but the top was up, so that despite the acres of leather Matt Remington was uncomfortably close.

'No,' he agreed. 'I thought it was—practical, though.'

There was silence for about a quarter of a mile, then he glanced at her and said with a lazy grin, 'I take it—from the dark looks I was on the receiving end of the other night—that you feel I . . . er . . . misled you back at Yamba.'

Kirra flushed, not only with annoyance at having her thoughts read so accurately, but because, as she'd been reflecting earlier, it might be a dubious standpoint to hold.

She said coolly, however, 'You did.'

'Do you think if you'd known who I was you'd have been more—circumspect?' he asked meditatively.

Kirra compressed her lips, then retorted, 'What I do know is that it was obviously more than practicality that prompted you to offer me this lift. A golden opportunity to pin me down and torment the life out of me, more like,' she finished bitterly.

He laughed quietly and said wryly, 'Not an easy

thing to do—pin you down, I mean. I gather Jeremy is having a similar problem.'

'Leave Jeremy out of this,' said Kirra tautly.

'So there is a "this",' he drawled.

'There isn't . . .' Kirra whispered.

He said softly, 'Strange you should say that when I can still remember the taste of your mouth and the feel of your body—so well.'

They had stopped at a set of lights and Kirra stared straight ahead, but the tell-tale colour had mounted in her cheeks again and a pulse at the base of her throat throbbed betrayingly.

'You tasted——' he began, but Kirra had heard enough.

'Don't!' she cried, and turned anguished blue-grey eyes on him. 'It could only have been a . . . an encounter for you, a few days perhaps, then we'd have gone our separate ways. I . . . I can understand how you feel, I *know* I behaved abominably, I admit that—but what else can I do?'

He lifted an eyebrow at her and put the car in gear as the lights changed and they moved off. 'You could explain why you behaved so badly,' he smiled, 'and explain at the same time why you're so sure it could have only been a passing encounter for me. A rather curious assumption,' he said drily.

'You appear to have eluded anything more permanent for quite some time.' The words were out, but no sooner had she said them than she regretted them and wondered what demon of malice or subconscious annoyance had prompted them.

'That could be merely a matter of not having found the right person—perhaps a subject you should give some thought to,' he said sardonically.

'It . . . I . . . oh, *hell*!' Kirra looked out of window rather blindly.

'Hell being a woman, you mean?'

'Yes,' she flashed at him because he was laughing at her again. 'What's more, I don't intend to say another word on the subject. Turn left here,' she commented haughtily. 'It's that building up the road, the first tall one.'

There was silence until he pulled the Rolls up and Kirra made to get out, but he put a hand out and grasped her wrist, saying, 'Oh, no, you don't. Not yet, sweetheart. If you refuse to explain, I don't see why I shouldn't have a go.'

'Let me go,' Kirra said through her teeth, her eyes flashing magnificently.

But it only seemed to amuse him, and he switched the interior light on and let his gaze wander over her insolently as he drawled, 'Yes, it seems to me it must be one of two things. Either you're one of those witless birds who go about chasing up a storm then retreating in a panic or, and personally this is my preference, dear Jeremy is so unsatisfactory in certain respects, you just can't help yourself from time to time.'

Kirra gasped, but he ignored her and went on thoughtfully, 'Which leads me to wonder if something once happened to you to make you decide on a marriage of *minds* to a chinless wonder who leaves you feeling like a bitch on heat.'

For a moment Kirra was so stunned that she could only stare at him with her mouth open. Then a red film of fury swam before her eyes, and she actually attempted to punch Matthew Remington in the mouth.

'You . . . you disgusting . . .' she sobbed, finding her other wrist now in his keeping. 'You . . .'

'Let me finish,' he said mildly. 'There are plenty of imperfect marriages, I'm sure, but for a hot-blooded girl like yourself, if you can't find the perfect bloke,' he smiled slightly, 'I'd go for the other thing.'

'I'm not.' Kirra wept tears of rage and revulsion. 'If only you knew . . .'

'But I do,' he pointed out, releasing her wrists aburptly.

Kirra put her hands to her face and was dimly astonished at the state she was in—sweating, crying, shaking.

'I hate you,' she whispered, suddenly galvanised into collecting all her belongings. 'Not only that, but I'm glad I did what I did, because in fact all I did was dent your pride, which must be a puny affair at the best of times. And if you must know, it nauseates me to think of you having *anything* to do with my parents. I also hope to God I never lay eyes on you again, but don't imagine I'll be leaving it entirely up to God!'

She opened the car door and risked one last blazing look at him, which was a mistake, because there was something in those hazel eyes that seemed to say—we'll see about that . . .

She was tempted to say—oh, no, we won't. But the look was gone and she contented herself with slamming the door on his grave, polite wish that she sleep well.

Nor was God or any of her own efforts any help to her as she stood in the foyer pressing the lift button imperatively, her eyes still blazing and her breasts heaving with anger. In fact, she might just as well have wasted her breath rather than make futile threats, as a tap on her shoulder revealed.

She swung round and it was Matt Remington holding her door keys, which must have fallen out of her bag during her furious scrabbling for her possessions.

'Don't say it,' he warned, as intense but conflicting expressions chased across her face—looks of rage and foolishness, hatred and a sinking sense of having made herself ridiculous. All of which combined to leave her speechless, without the benefit of his warning, but she did try to snatch the keys from him—a mistake.

He closed his fist around them and said softly, his eyes gleaming wickedly, 'Temper, temper, my dear Kirra. Do you always allow your emotions such free rein?'

For an instant Kirra had the greatest difficulty in not bursting into tears. But the effort was so great that it left her drained; her shoulders slumped wearily and she closed her eyes—all of which, she told herself time and time again afterwards, was a tactical error of huge proportions, because it allowed Matt Remington to have his way with her, without her even putting up a fight.

She did, at the first feel of his arms sliding around her, open her eyes disbelievingly, and she certainly parted her lips, but it was a faint, husky sound of protest that came forth. Even that died as she stared up into his half-closed eyes and saw the flickering smile that played on his lips before his mouth covered hers.

But when the kiss ended she was curiously shaky on her legs, and had to bear the indignity of his keeping an arm around her shoulders while he summoned the lift—it had come and gone again during the interim. Then he handed her in, handed her the keys and stepped back with a mocking little salute as the doors started to close, a wordless gesture that somehow shouted its meaning loud and clear.

'No,' Kirra breathed, staring at the closed doors, realising that somone must have summoned the lift from above, and that for a distraught moment she couldn't even remember her floor. 'No . . . I didn't kiss you back, it wasn't anything like that. You were just too clever, and I was quite unprepared —which I'll never be again.'

She woke in the middle of the night, however, shaking and sweating again because in her dreams she'd relived the feel of his arms around her, of his tall, strong body against hers, of that almost insolently slow kiss.

By the morning she knew, though, that she hated Matt Remington more than ever, if that were possible—hated him because he probably could, and probably did at will, arouse many women with his expertise. But of all the things he'd done to her and said to her, what she hated him for most were his comments about Jeremy. I could kill him for that, she thought coldly.

She spent the week almost comfortably cocooned by her sense of outrage, so much so that, when the blow fell, she didn't recognise it immediately. In fact, it was only by chance that she was paging through the business section of the paper at all, trying to locate the advertisement for an estate auction said to be offering some interesting antique porcelain, when a smallish headline caught her eye . . . 'Condiment Conundrum'.

She almost didn't read it, and even when she did the veiled speculation of the article concerning the future of a carefully unnamed condiment company merely caused her to grimace and think ruefully that it would mean one less competitor for Munro's.

But half a minute later, still leafing through the paper, her heart suddenly started to pound and her mouth went dry; she visualised her father who was looking oddly tired these days, and the way her parents were almost—courting?—yes, courting Matthew Remington, who was such a rich man and in a related business . . .

'No,' she whispered, her eyes suddenly horrified. 'Oh God, no. Please tell me it's not so!'

'But why didn't you *tell* me?' she said almost frantically to her parents, standing before them as they sat side by side in their beautiful living-room that evening, holding hands.

'Darling, I did want to,' Naomi said gently. 'But your father felt it would be . . . well he didn't want to burden you with this when you rather obviously were . . .' She hesitated.

'So wrapped up in myself—I must have been blind,' Kirra said bitterly. 'Oh, forgive me—oh, Dad . . . Mum . . .'

After an emotional few minutes, Kirra recovered a bit and her father endeavoured to explain what had happened.

'It was mostly my fault.'

'Dad . . .'

'But it was, Kirra. I got out of step with things

—I thought it was enough for Munro's to rest on its name and reputation. But now a large part of the market has been captured by opposition companies, more innovative, advertising-orientated ones, and for some time now I've been pouring capital into the company which I might just as well have poured down the drain.'

'There's the house,' Kirra said quickly, 'and my apartment, anything . . .'

'Kirra, that's what we're down to now. It's all we have left to pay off our creditors, and it's just not enough to emerge from this débâcle honourably, I'm afraid.'

Kirra sprang up. 'But . . .'

Her mother spoke soothingly. 'We've tried everything, darling, but the financial climate is against us, as well as everything else. But we do have one last hope—Matt Remington. All is not lost yet, love. If your father can persuade him to sink enough money into the company for Munro's to make a comeback we still have the name.'

'How?' Kirra's voice trembled. 'I mean . . . how did you get on to him?'

'One of his companies manufactures glass bottles and is our largest creditor,' her father said. 'He's also a rather brilliant business entrepreneur, and if anyone can save Munro's, he can. Hopefully, as a creditor, it will appeal to him from the point of view of minimising his company's losses as well.'

Kirra groaned.

'Pet,' her father said anxiously.

'I just wish you'd told me,' she whispered. 'That night he came to dinner . . .'

'That was your mother's idea. She thought it

would help to present us as a family.'

'I've always believed in the power of personalities over cold, hard figures,' Naomi said wryly. 'And I did want to tell Kirra then, Kenneth, but you wouldn't let me,' she added with for her an unusual touch of asperity. 'I just hope that one day you'll realise your womenfolk are capable of bearing burdens, too!'

'I do now,' Sir Kenneth said, his eyes softening as they rested on his wife. 'You've been wonderful! As for you, my dear,' he turned to Kirra, 'you more than compensated last Sunday for any deficiencies at the dinner party. But let's not kid ourselves,' he sobered, 'in this kind of deal, it is going to be cold, hard facts and figures that count.'

Kirra flinched inwardly and thought, I wonder? She said quickly, 'So he hasn't made a decision yet?'

'No, but I've given him *carte blanche* with the books and the plant, and he's promised me one within a week.'

'I see.'

'Kirra,' her mother looked at her anxiously, 'won't you stay the night? You look so pale, darling, but whatever, we'll survive somehow. Perhaps we could become romantic nomads and live in a tent.'

Kirra stayed with them for the evening, but declined to stay the night. And once again, as she drove home, her mind was in a turmoil. So many thoughts, such as how it had never occured to her that her father might not have inherited *his* father's business acumen—after all, he was an acknowledged master strategist in a military sense. Yet now she wondered—and wondered with a pang why she'd never thought of it before—whether his heart and soul had ever been in the world of business, or hot sauces, French dressings and chutneys. But worst of all was the thought of her own blithe acceptance of all her parents had bestowed upon her, and the way she'd been so selfishly wrapped up in her own problems that she had not even sensed something was wrong.

Then she put her knuckles to her mouth and forced herself to think of Matt Remington, and to wonder how cold, hard figures would really stand up against the insults she had offered him, the things she'd said . . . more than enough to ensure that her beloved father went to the wall.

And she completed the drive home with tears streaming down her cheeks and the most painful question mark she'd ever endured printed on her mind.

CHAPTER FOUR

THE reception-room Kirra sat in the next morning was quietly but luxuriously furnished, and the door through which she'd come was marked with his name—in gold lettering, just the sight of which had been enough to make her heart beat with fright—and an impressive list of companies below.

Then it had taken her some time to persuade the pretty young receptionist that Mr Remington would see Miss Munro even without an appointment if only she would pass on the name. Not that Kirra had been at all as sure of this as she had sounded, but finally the girl had lifted the phone and spoken hesitantly into it.

Nor had Kirra missed the spark of speculation in her eyes, as she had replaced the phone and said, 'Mr Remington will see you, Miss Munro, if you don't mind waiting.'

Which was what she doing now, flipping unseeingly through trade journals, growing more tense and nervous by the minute, more convinced she was doing the wrong thing and equally convinced that he was deliberately keeping her waiting.

Now he knows you're here, it can only look ridiculous if you back out, she told herself fretfully, but how lucky—trying for a lighter note—you had the forethought to ask for the whole day off.

Nothing lightened her sense of doom though,

and she restlessly smoothed the straight skirt of the grey linen summer suit she wore with navy-blue accessories.

She had chosen the outfit deliberately because it was the most businesslike one she possessed, and would, she hoped, banish some of the other impressions Matthew Remington no doubt had of her. But she knew there were shadows beneath her eyes, testimony to a sleepless night, although she didn't know that they added considerably to the pretty young receptionist's pleasurable curiosity as to the nature of Kirra's call on her boss. Or that she had just decided Kirra must be in love with him— something she had been unable to avoid herself from afar—and was losing him. Then a bleeper sounded beside her and she rose and told Kirra, with infinite sympathy, that Mr Remington would see her now.

Kirra followed her with a faint frown of surprise, but forgot all else as the girl opened a door and stood aside, 'Miss Munro, Mr Remington.'

Matt Remington didn't rise. Instead, he took off a pair of gold-rimmed glasses and sat back in his chair as Kirra stepped into the room and stopped, pressing her suddenly sweating palms to her sides.

Then he said drily, 'This is a surprise, Kirra. Sit down.'

She sat as she'd been trained to do, with a straight back, her hands clasped loosely and her ankles crossed, and glanced across the wide, paper-laden desk between them to see that he was waiting expressionlessly. She swallowed and, with a queer little sigh, said, 'I don't know where to begin.'

'Do you ever?' he asked with irony.

She coloured and bit her lip, wondering with

some irony herself where all her fire had gone. But this was something quite different and totally intimidating—this was like confronting a different man, a man to whom the kisses he had accepted or stolen meant nothing. But then, I almost knew that, she thought shakily. I just didn't know the kind of power he could wield. Now I do . . .

She licked her lips as he waited with an eyebrow raised coolly. Then he said, 'Perhaps I can assist you. You know, don't you? Did your parents finally decide to tell you?'

'No,' she said huskily. 'I read something in the paper and . . . confronted them.'

'Bravo, Kirra! And you've even gone one step further—you've come here to ask me to save Munro's. How brave. Do they know you're here?'

Kirra took a breath and flinched at the detachment in his eyes and voice despite his words. 'No,' she said very quietly, 'and I've actually come only to ask . . . to ask you not to let what . . . happened between us, influence you. It would be . . .'

'You thought I might?' he broke in.

'I don't know what to think,' she said unevenly, feeling, with a cold, sinking sense of certainty, that it had been a terrible mistake to come.

'Oh, I think you do,' he said softly. 'Wouldn't it give you great pleasure to point out how heartless I'd be if I discontinued my nauseating contact with your parents in the light of what you now know? Do you know,' he looked at her dispassionately and continued thoughtfully, 'if you'd come here today and offered to . . . er . . . take up with me where you once left off, anything to save your parents from bankruptcy, I might have preferred it. Not that I'd have accepted . . . But you've played the wrong tune, again, sweetheart.'

'I didn't mean it to sound the way you made it . . .'

'Of course you did,' he said indifferently.

'All right, what if I did?' she retorted bitterly. 'As for the other tune,' her eyes flashed scathingly, 'I can just imagine how you would have gloated. And while we're on the subject, do you come out of all this smelling like a rose, Mr Matthew Remington, professional wanderer turned business magnate? Just how long, I wonder, would you have enjoyed taking me in, the way you did——' She broke off and put a hand to her mouth.

'So we're back to that,' he said with a grin. 'Has it occurred to you that perhaps we *both* were somewhat evasive? Also, that it suited your poor-little-rich-girl frame of mind to build a romantic daydream about a man you found camping somewhere?'

'I'm not a poor . . .'

'You did say you felt . . . hemmed in. I know now it wasn't anything to with Munro's. As for being a poor little rich girl—in the mixed-up sense of the phrase—why else would your parents be afraid to tell you about this disaster that's befallen them?' His hazel eyes flicked her contemptuously.

Kirra flinched and reddened.

'Then there's Jeremy still dangling on his string.'

Kirra straightened and gritted her teeth. 'If . . . if you've quite finished, I'll go. But you're wrong about one thing. The only reason I came to see you *was* for my parents, and I didn't . . .' She groped for words, swallowed, then looked straight at him and said very quietly, 'Is it too late to . . . *beg* you to change your mind for their sake?'

He didn't answer immediately, but studied her expressionlessly. Then he swung his chair round to stare out of the window briefly. 'There is one way we could bargain about this, Kirra.' He swung back and looked at her with narrowed eyes.

Kirra was seized with an insane premonition, then she thought, no, he said he wouldn't . . . but what?

She rushed into speech. 'I'd sell everything I possess,' she offered eagerly. 'My apartment, my car, my jewellery . . .'

His lips quirked. 'Do you think that much would save Munro's? And how would you live?'

She shrugged. 'It might help. And I'm not quite as hopeless as you appear to imagine. I do have a career to support me,' she added with dignity.

'What do you do?'

'I work for a firm of interior decorators.'

'Are you an interior decorator?'

'I did a course,' she said stiffly. 'What's wrong with that?' she asked at his wry look.

'Nothing! Very . . . proper,' he commented, making her feel as if she couldn't have chosen a more idle, frivolous career. 'But what do you actually do?'

'I collect *objets d'art* for the firm. I have a fair reputation for a keen eye and a sense of values,' she said defiantly, uncaring if she'd allowed a prickle of hostility to break through her defences again. Because . . . oh hell, she thought, with a sudden bleak look which didn't escape him.

He smiled gently. 'Very commendable, Kirra. But the money in itself would be like a drop in the ocean, and anyway, it wasn't what I had in mind.'

She moved abruptly. 'I have nothing else to offer.'

'Not entirely. You have yourself.'

She froze, then said through stiff lips, 'I don't think I heard you right.'

He raised an eyebrow. 'Yes, you did, Kirra.'

'But you said,' she burst out, 'just now you said . . .' She couldn't go on.

He sat back. 'That was something different.'

'What do you mean? Forgive me, but I got the distinct impression we were discussing the exchange of my body for your intervention to save Munro's,' she said, her voice rising.

His lips twitched and the old amusement was back in his eyes. 'Plain speaking, Kirra,' he said quizzically.

She jumped up. 'No, it is not, damn it! What do you mean if you don't . . .' She stopped because she was quivering in every nerve, and it was like a nightmare, this, and at any moment she would start screaming like a fishwife at him. 'What do you mean?' she asked through her teeth.

'I was talking about taking possession of your . . . beautiful body, honourably, dear Kirra,' he said almost lazily, 'in exchange for my intervention to save Munro's. I was talking about marrying you.' He smiled faintly as her mouth dropped open and her eyes almost fell out on stalks. 'It's a very old idea, you know,' he added conversationally. 'Daughters, especially beautiful ones, have been a form of barter for centuries. And the more beautiful, the more valuable.'

Kirra stared at him, dumbfounded, then groped her way back to her chair. 'I don't believe this,' she said weakly. 'I . . . we're not living in the Dark Ages. And if you imagine my father would *dream* . . . I told you, he has no idea I'm here!'

'The thought never entered my head. I'm sure your father would be horrified, although,' he shrugged, 'he could even feel relieved to know you're . . . safe. But I thought you might like to make the gesture yourself if it does mean so much to you not to see your father go to the wall.'

'Safe?' Kirra said faintly, feeling suddenly dizzy and ill. 'Safe,' she repeated, 'with a man who has blackmailed me into marrying him, who doesn't even *like* me, who thinks I'm a mixed-up freak?'

'Actually, Kirra,' he interrupted, sitting up and looking amused again, 'perhaps I should remind you that here are some things we like very much about each other.' His hazel gaze lingered on her mouth, then dropped to the curve of her breasts beneath the linen jacket.

'Oh,' she said despairingly, her cheeks burning, and she dropped her head into her hands. 'I don't believe this. Anyway, I'm *engaged*.'

'So you keep telling me,' he said derisively. 'However, without even having met Jeremy, I don't think he's the right one for you, Kirra—but then I've mentioned that before. And don't ask me why I have this conviction, because I should have thought it was obvious.'

Kirra raised suddenly tearful eyes to Matt Remington across the desk. 'I hate you for . . . what you've implied about Jeremy,' she said huskily. 'He's worth ten of you. He . . . he's the nicest man I know, and I love him.'

Their gazes caught and held, and when Matt spoke it was on a different note altogether. 'Perhaps you've confused warmth and friendship—which I'm not knocking, but it's a different thing from a true, total commitment between a man and a woman.'

Kirra caught her breath and felt as if her heart had been pierced by an arrow . . . of truth? She whispered, 'How can you say that? How can you talk about a true, total commitment, when you're trying to force me to marry you for . . . revenge?'

'Kirra,' he said, reverting to that lazy, conversational tone, 'I can guarantee that within six weeks of marrying me, you'll have forgotten all about things like revenge and barter.'

'Oh! Of all the . . . *oh!*' was all she could manage to say.

'As for true and total,' he went on, seemingly unperturbed by her furious, frustrated agitation, 'we have a lot to build on. We're physically,' he said softly, 'rather . . . spontaneously attracted to each other, wouldn't you say? When we don't let other things intrude, we've even been known to enjoy each other's company.'

'For one day!'

'A lot can happen in a day.' His eyes glinted.

Kirra put a hand to her head helplessly. 'But *marriage* . . .'

'You did point out to me recently that I'd eluded it for too long.'

'I didn't say *that* . . .'

He raised a quizzical eyebrow at her. 'I quite got the impression you felt rather bitter about it, though.'

'I . . .' Kirra closed her mouth, then she tried again. 'You're not . . . you can't really be serious.'

'I am,' he assured her blandly.

'But there's nothing I could bring you.' She trailed off and coloured brightly at the mocking little smile twisting his lips. 'All right,' she said stiffly then, 'but when that *palls*, what then?'

'If it palls,' he murmured, 'we'll do what most couple do—who have a vested interest in each other.'

'But don't you see?' she cried. 'What possible vested interest could you have in me once you're not interested in sleeping with me?'

'Oh,' he drawled, 'by that time we'll probably have started a family. I shall certainly accord you the . . . respect due the mother of my children.'

Kirra stared at him, speechless.

'Incidentally, that's where some of the things you could bring me will come in. Despite your rather pathetic confusion on the subject of men, dear Kirra, you have a certain kind of class—and a very famous name to go with it. My background,' he paused, 'has become a little tarnished. So I can assure you that if you play your part, our . . . arrangement will be . . .'

'I don't believe I'm hearing this,' she broke in faintly.

He shrugged and flicked her with a dispassionate glance that said all too clearly, take it or leave it.

'When,' she licked her lips, 'do I have to make up my mind?'

'The sooner the better. I'd hate to get the feeling I was doing all this work,' he gestured at the papers on the desk, 'for nothing,' he said softly.

'But . . . if I hadn't come here today,' she stared at him in anguish, 'what would you have done then?'

'My dear Kirra, I always knew you would come, if not today . . .'

'But say I hadn't found out until you *had* made a decision one way or the other!'

'You wouldn't have remained in ignorance much longer.'

'You disgust me,' she whispered.

He grinned. 'I can foresee some lively times between us, Kirra,' he said.

Her nostrils flared and she pinched her lips into a thin line. 'How soon is the sooner the better?' she asked through her teeth.

'Let's see,' he glanced at the diary on his desk, 'despite so much being at stake, you should have a little time to consider, it, I guess. Why don't you invite me to dinner tomorrow night? We could, if you are so minded, hammer out the details.'

Kirra closed her eyes again, this time because she felt she was in danger of fainting from sheer rage and disbelief. But somehow or other she found the composure to stand up and say crisply, 'Very well, shall we say—seven-thirty?'

'Seven-thirty will be fine.' He stood up himself and came round the desk to her. 'There is one other thing. It would be wiser if you'd . . . disengaged yourself from Jeremy before you consent to marry me.'

'*Consent*?' she hissed.

'Or whichever way you care to look at it,' he replied mildly. 'And if you don't agree with me that it's long overdue in its own right, if you know what I mean, why don't you try thinking back to Lover's Point? In fact,' he lifted a hand and trailed his fingertips down the side of her face, 'thinking back might just help you make the right decisions all round. For once.'

'Oh, do you think so?' she retorted, moving out of his reach. 'I prefer to think forward.'

He leant back against the desk and folded his

arms thoughtfully. 'Tell me about him.'

'Who?'

'The first man in your life—I assume there was at least one other apart from Jeremy—and now me.'

'He's dead.' Kirra stopped and bit her lip. 'I don't have the slightest intention of telling you about him—it's none of your business, for one thing,' she added with a rising tide of frustration in her voice.

'It could be that everything about you will soon be my business,' he said with a mocking little smile.

'I . . . I . . . oh hell!' she whispered. 'Just let me get out of here!'

He straightened. 'There's nothing stopping you. Until tomorrow night, then.' And he strolled across the room and opened the door for her.

She stood where she was, rooted to the spot and staring at him helplessly, a gaze he returned enigmatically, then with a glint of amusement in his hazel eyes. And finally he said with a glance at his watch, 'I'm afraid I have another appointment in about ten minutes, Kirra. Sorry, but . . .'

'Oh!' she breathed and glared at him, then swept past him without another word, her head held high. Not high enough to miss his wry grin, however.

The next evening was breathless and humid, although great banks of cloud had built up out to sea, promising reviving showers, but tantalisingly staying out at sea.

At twenty past seven, Kirra stood in the middle of her lounge, confident that everything was ready—that was all she was confident of. That her apartment looked its best, polished and gleaming, that dinner was taken care of and that she looked her best. Why it was so important to her to present this image, she wasn't sure.

She wore a slim, ivory, waistless dress with padded shoulders, very short sleeves and a V-neckline; at her neck was a two-strand pearl choker set with a square topaz that had a tinge of blue fire in its depths. She had been to the hairdresser that afternoon, and her dark hair gleamed beneath the light like a well-mannered fall of heavy silk, framing her face and just brushing her shoulders. She'd even had a manicure, something she normally did herself; but it wasn't her perfectly painted oval nails that caused her to look at her hands frequently, it was the lack of Jeremy's ring. And, each time she did, a feeling of pain pierced her heart.

Coming home from work, she'd invested a small fortune in a new perfume, new for her but a very famous one; and for considerably less, she had bought a bunch of pink chrysanthemums.

What she had not done, despite laying down these battle-lines—and it had struck her at the last minute that this poised, groomed and perfumed version of herself was a bit incongruous, but then consoled herself that she desperately needed poise at least—what she had not done, was come up with an actual plan of battle. In fact, she was all too acutely aware that she couldn't really bring herself to believe Matthew Remington intended to force the issue. She was living in the hope that she would discover tonight that it had been a hoax—surely it had to be! He could have virtually any woman he chose, so why her—and why like this?

She sighed and her hall clock chimed seven-thirty just as the doorbell rang. She took a deep breath and attempted to wipe all emotion from her expression as she went to answer it.

For a moment they just gazed at each other, Kirra unaware that she'd not been totally successful about removing a last glint of hostility from her blue-grey gaze; Matt Remington looking austere and inscrutable in a dark suit and a plain white shirt.

Then she realised he was carrying a gold foil-topped bottle in one hand and a bunch of creamy rosebuds in the other. 'Roses! And champagne,' she murmured. 'How kind! Do come in. You're the first man I know to do that.'

He raised a sceptical eyebrow. 'I should have thought I'd joined a long queue.'

'I meant—brought flowers by hand, not sent them,' she said defensively.

'Then I'm glad I did,' he replied. 'In years to come, we can treasure it as one of the first "firsts" of our relationship.'

Kirra tightened her lips, but took the flowers and champagne from him. 'Make yourself at home while I deal with these,' she said tautly.

When she brought the roses back in a vase, he was standing in the middle of her lounge with his back to her, his hands in his pockets, staring at the darkened view through the open sliding doors. He turned as she put the vase down, and as she straightened he said, 'You're looking stunning, Kirra.'

'Thank you. Would you like a drink? And can I take your jacket?'

'Yes, thanks, on both counts,' he replied

politely, and for a few minutes, while Kirra busied herself with these formalities, he looked around her lounge and dining alcove.

She'd decorated them herself in a blend of styles, that worked surprisingly well. The walls were a pale, smoky grey, and the dining-table and occasional tables were lacquered a slightly bluer grey, had smoked glass tops and were all of a sleek, spare design. The spareness stopped there, however. Two deep, comfortable couches upholstered in wistaria-blue linen faced each other across a big, low glass table that stood on a dusky pink and soft blue close-textured rug. The pink was repeated in cushions on the couches and lampshades, and the table bore a lot of her favourite things: her beaten silver statue of a Chinese coolie, her plaited straw horse, a glazed pottery dish. There were also books, magazines and the chrysanthemums she had bought that afternoon in a stubby crystal vase.

Matt Remington came out of his contemplation of her room as she handed him his drink, and said, 'Very nice, Kirra.'

'I'm glad you approve,' she said with some irony, prompted not only by a desire to show him she didn't need his approval, but because he looked disturbingly tall and oddly at home in his shirt sleeves and with his tie loosened. If I'd known he was going to look so at ease, I'd have let him stifle in his jacket, she thought darkly.

'Were these sent?' he asked idly, touching the fluffy pink heads of the chrysanthemums with his long fingers, and curiously transmitting the feel of those soft, cool, tightly packed petals to her fingertips.

'No. I bought those to ch——' She stopped

'To cheer yourself up?'

'Yes,' she said baldly.

He studied her taut expression silently, then his gaze slid to her left hand and he lifted an eyebrow and said softly, 'So you did it.'

'*Yes* . . . I mean . . .'

He waited.

Kirra clenched her teeth. 'I didn't do it because of you—other than in the sense that I might be in no position to be engaged to another man.'

'Why *did* you do it, then?' he asked, a slight smile twisting his lips.

She took a sip of her drink, then shrugged and sighed. 'In the end, I didn't—he did,' she said bleakly. 'He came to see me last night, and when I started to say something he . . .' She stopped and blinked.

'Go on,' Matt said quietly.

'He said he'd known for a while I was unhappy and . . . confused, and it had to be because I wasn't ready to marry him. He . . .' her voice shook, 'said he was releasing me from our engagement because he'd come to understand I wasn't for him. If you've any idea how bad that made me feel . . .'

'Perhaps,' Matt said absently. 'All the same, I'm glad it happened that way, because it means Jeremy understood you. If you weren't in this predicament, you'd probably be feeling relieved.'

Kirra stared at him, desperately wanting to contradict him.

Why don't we sit down?' he murmured, and his hazel eyes glinted at the way she tossed her head in sudden fury, but she sat all the same.

He sat down opposite her and stretched his arm along the back of the settee, while Kirra, battling once more for composure, found herself staring at him again, incredulously this time and also wondering a little helplessly how she could restore him to the quiet stranger who had taken out her splinter on Lover's Point. I should have known he could be like this, she thought. It's all there if you know what to look for: the self-assurance, the plain dynamic arrogance of that superb body, which his beautifully tailored clothes, if anything, enhance, the intelligence in his eyes and sometimes the wry cynicism in the twist of those well-cut lips . . . the way you just *know* he's expert at pleasing women and . . . and despising them . . .

She took a jolting little breath as he looked up suddenly and his hazel gaze clashed with hers. But not me, please don't let me . . . how could I possibly be attracted *now*? her thoughts continued feverishly.

'You were thinking?' he drawled.

'I . . . yes, I was.' She forced herself to sound cool and dispassionate. 'I was wondering when you were going to end this farce, as a matter of fact.'

'Which farce?' he queried.

Kirra smoothed her skirt, then hoped he hadn't noticed how her hand had trembled. 'The one you referred to earlier as the *predicament* I find myself in now,' she said, and couldn't resist adding, 'Don't you think you've got enough mileage out of it?'

'Mileage?' he repeated. 'No—because it's no farce, Kirra. Either you marry me or your parents go bankrupt. In my terminology, that's what you call a deal, not a . . .'

'A deal?' she interrupted scathingly. 'I hesitate to disagree with you, but in anyone's terminology it's nothing but a plan to avenge yourself and humiliate me!'

'Kirra, you've said all that,' he reminded her lazily. 'Let's not repeat ourselves. Is there no . . . new ground you'd like to cover?'

Kirra closed her eyes and put a hand to her mouth. Then she said abruptly, 'All right. I can't understand why it has to be marriage. Wouldn't . . . blackmailing me into being your . . . mistress,' she swallowed suddenly and looked away, 'be even more satisfactory, if anything?'

Matt sat forward with his glass cradled in his hands, contemplating it, then he looked up and across at her with a devilish glint of mockery in his eyes. 'Are you offering yourself for that position?'

She said hastily, 'No . . . well . . .'

He waited, then smiled faintly. 'Let's see if I can read your mind. Did it occur to you as a viable alternative? Did you picture yourself as a martyr to the cause?'

'Stop it,' she whispered.

He sat back. 'Then you weren't, as a last-ditch effort, planning to offer me a less permanent and purely sexual proposition—I'm glad of that, Kirra. You would have found it impossible to carry through, you know.'

'*You* . . .' her cheeks were flushed hectically and her blue-grey eyes dark with first, naked embarrassment because he had read her mind, then a raging desire to demolish him, 'you *really* think you're God's gift to women, don't you? How was I ever so taken in?'

He grimaced. 'You didn't seem to mind my . . . talent at lovemaking once, and I'm sorry if it bothers you now, but I think you'll appreciate it in the end, Kirra.'

'Oh——' It was more a groan of disbelief and despair and she stood up convulsively. 'I . . . let's have dinner before I'm sick! I suppose it's no good appealing to your gentlemanly instincts.'

'I'm afraid not,' he said softly, looking up at her, his eyes gleaming now with something she couldn't decipher—unless it was laughter. 'Can I give you a hand?'

'No.' She frowned suddenly and started to say something, but changed her mind and walked away into the kitchen. But, as she started to dish up the first course, there was a question mark in her mind. *Was* he serious?

She fed him plump little oysters in their shells, rare roast beef with baked potatoes and fresh green beans, and a fruit salad spiked with Marsala and served with whipped cream.

And all through the meal she followed his lead obediently, which was to converse easily and impersonally. Not, she thought once, that she achieved anything like that famous—or was it infamous?—ease of Lover's Point, but she did her best—she couldn't think what else to do, and it had struck her, anyway, that if she could be normal she might have a better chance of unravelling some of the things she simply didn't understand about him. It wasn't until his remarks at the conclusion of the meal that she also realised she was still hoping it was all a bad dream.

He said, 'That was great. You have the makings of a first-class hostess—did I mention that once we're married I intend to set up a more . . . prolific social life than I've lived until now? More respectably prolific, at least,' he added with umistakable irony.

Kirra stared at him over the fruit salad.

'With a big house to match—I suppose you'd rather be based here than Melbourne or Sydney?'

She licked her lips. 'I think . . . I hear the coffee perking. Will you excuse me for a moment? We . . . we'll have it in the lounge.'

'Of course.'

She did more than make the coffee. She went into her bedroom and freshened her lipstick, brushed her hair and sprayed on some more perfume. Then she leant her forehead against the mirror and whispered, 'Please God, don't let this be happening to me.'

He was sitting in the lounge when she returned with the coffee-tray. She poured two cups from an elegant silver pot, asked him if he'd like a liqueur, which he declined, and finally there was nothing to do but sit down opposite him again and try to put her thoughts into words.

'C-could I ask you a favour?' she said haltingly.

'Go ahead.' He ran a hand through his thick, fair hair and stirred his coffee.

'If I ask you some questions, will you answer them honestly?'

He looked up. 'Yes.'

'Is . . .' Kirra hesitated, then took the plunge, 'is there some reason I'm not aware of for all this?'

'What do you mean?'

'Some reason why you're marrying a woman you basically despise, instead of . . . a woman you love, someone you could share a true and total commitment with? I mean,' she said huskily. 'those were your own words, so you must be aware that it's possible, that it exists.'

'As you were when you got engaged to Jeremy?' he countered coolly.

She flushed slightly, but said steadily, 'My mistakes were made in good faith—oh, perhaps foolishly, but at least there was, with Jeremy anyway, affection. This, us, doesn't even have to redeem it, and please don't quote what happened at Lover's Point to me again. Let's look at it from other angles or cover new ground if you prefer. I'm . . . a little tired of figuring as a . . . witless bird, or if not that, a bitch on heat,' she said deliberately.

His lips twitched. 'I apologise for that one.'

She looked him straight in the eye, then went on, 'Have you no faith in finding a woman to love?'

He was silent for a time. Then, 'You wanted me to be honest—no.'

Kirra shivered, and he noted it with a narrowing of his eyes. 'That disturbs you,' he murmured.

'Yes,' she agreed. 'I also find it a bit difficult to fit in with your . . . sermonising to me.'

'I don't go around leading people on,' he said quietly.

Kirra bit her lip, then surprised herself, 'Perhaps it's only through making some mistakes that you . . . expose the right emotions.'

He smiled coolly. 'Perhaps. Unless you get buried in the quicksand of the wrong ones.'

'So, you're not prepared to take the chance of that happening?' she queried.

'Were you?' Kirra hesitated. 'Perhaps I should tell you that your mother has favoured me with a brief version of your first engagement, Kirra,' he said reflectively. 'A fortune-hunter by the name of . . . Bret, I believe it was.'

Kirra paled and inwardly cursed her beloved mother.

'Wouldn't you say,' he continued softly, 'that Jeremy was your hedge against that ever happening to you again?'

'We're still . . . All right,' she conceded, 'that makes us even, *both* afraid of being hurt again—am I right?'

He shrugged and said amusedly, 'You've obviously heard about my father and . . .'

'So it was true,' she broke in.

'Oh, it was true all right. However, and I'm sorry to have to disappoint you if you were imagining I'm making you the object of all my cynicism on the subject, but I got over it years ago. I was only twenty-one at the time, she was older, and I was undoubtedly going through that period when older women are fatally fascinating.'

'Then why *are* you so cynical?' Kirra burst out. 'There has to be a reason, and don't try and tell me you're not!'

'I wouldn't dream of it,' he drawled. 'As for why, I think I honestly believe it's all a bag of moonshine. There are . . . attractions between men and women, friendships, but,' he looked at her meditatively, 'to quote the King of Siam if I may, "all the rest you hear is fairy-tale".'

Kirra sat transfixed for a moment, then she dropped her head into her hands.

'Which is why,' he went on after a moment, 'a sound business proposition with a dash of the physical thrown in, serves one much better, I think. For all concerned. And you'd be amazed at the number of women who agree with me.'

'*Agree* with you?' It was a hollow, muffled whisper.

'Why, yes. Since I made a lot of money, they've

actually been flocking to my door with business propositions, all manner of propositions.'

Kirra lifted her head. 'You can't accuse me of that,' she said hoarsely.

He smiled gently and said pensively, 'You did come to me with *something* on your mind, if you remember. Nor would we be having this conversation if I didn't have the money to redeem your parents.'

'Wouldn't we? This was all *your* idea.'

He thought for a bit, then said with a flash of amusement, 'You're right. You know, I do think I was getting a bit jaded and your . . . blow hot, blow cold approach was rather novel—it'll certainly add a bit of spice to the proceedings if you can keep it up, but I guess what really appealed to me was the opportunity to turn the tables for once.'

It occurred to Kirra that he wasn't serious, that he couldn't be, and she made one last effort. 'Do you . . . honestly believe it doesn't exist?' she whispered. 'Have you never seen two people in love, still in love after years of marriage?'

He stood up after a moment and walked over to the open sliding doors. 'Yes, I've seen it,' he said in a different voice. 'Recently, too. In fact, you're the living product of one such case, but how many do you see? One in a thousand?' He shrugged and turned. 'The rest of us do the best we can. Why don't you stop floundering around and say yes, Kirra?'

'Because I just can't believe . . .'

'Believe it,' he said drily. 'Look at it as one of life's nasty little surprises, if you like. Despite your—tangled love-affairs, you've had a charmed life up until now, but very few people escape life unscathed. How much *do* your parents mean to you?'

Kirra looked away, and thought of her father hearing that his last chance of emerging honourably from this débâcle had gone. She thought of her mother being so bright and brave, and how she'd failed them by being totally unaware in their hour of need. She remembered the crisis days after Bret when, although she'd spurned their advice, they'd lovingly helped her to pick up the pieces.

'All right—if you put it that way, yes.'

'Good,' he said unemotionally. 'How about a drink now? You look as if you could do with it.'

'Is that . . . all you can say?' she asked incredulously.

'What did you expect? That I'd go down on my knees and . . .'

'Oh . . .' Kirra jumped up and went to sweep past him, but he caught her wrist.

'On the other hand, if I thought you weren't going to fight me and only exhaust yourself and work yourself up into a state of hysteria . . . we could do this.' He released her wrist and pulled her into his arms, his hazel eyes glinting with mockery as he studied her outraged expression and felt the way she tensed convulsively.

'But then again,' he said very softly, his lips barely moving, 'that's half the charm of you, Kirra. The pleasure I'm going to get . . . taming the shrew.'

'You're . . . a devil,' Kirra hissed, 'and don't imagine I won't fight you.'

'I never did—well, not since we re-encountered one another. So fight away, my beautiful brideto-be, I expect no less.'

Kirra closed her eyes and deliberately went limp in his arms, but her lashes flew up as she heard him laugh softly; then he picked her up and carried her over to the settee, where he set her down lengthwise on it, pushed a cushion behind her shoulders, and sat down beside her on the edge. 'I should warn you,' he murmured, pulling her skirt down over her knees, which she pressed together immediately, causing his lips to twitch, 'that passivity is a really hard act to maintain against a lover with a . . . slow hand and all the time in the world.'

Their eyes clashed, and to her horror Kirra felt a tinge of pink steal into her cheeks and her nerve-ends start to tingle, almost in anticipation of that slow hand. Her lips parted and the pulse at the base of her throat just above the blue fire topaz fluttered.

He observed all this with a narrowing of his eyes, and his face set in rather harsh lines, somehow remote and austere, and Kirra could feel herself shrinking beneath the weight of what she had unwittingly given away, like a flower fading and shrivelling.

He said then, with his hazel eyes completely un-readable, 'Unfortunately I don't have all the time in the world, so you're quite safe tonight—don't look so tragic.'

Kirra clamped her lips on the sob of despair and frustration that rose to her lips as she wondered if there was anything with which to dent his casual, supremely male arrogance.

'You were going to say?' he asked.

She forced herself to speak. 'Nothing—except, what does happen now?'

'We could make some plans.'

She struggled into a sitting position, bending her knees and pushing off her ivory kid shoes as the high heels dug into the upholstery. Her hair swung forward and she lifted a hand to tuck it behind her ear. She licked her lips, no longer painted petal pink, and looked at him at last, her blue-grey eyes shadowed and equally unreadable now. 'If you like. I don't quite see how we're going to spring this on my parents.'

'We won't. We'll lead up to it gradually. So long as it's a fact when the final papers are signed.'

'How long will that be?'

He shrugged. 'Time enough. There are contracts to draw up. In the meantime, it might be an idea to have some sort of a party to announce the merger. We could demonstrate our . . . shall we say, burgeoning interest in each other.'

'Start setting the scene, do you mean?' she said huskily.

He smiled faintly. 'Something like that.'

'Very well. Would you mind . . . I'm really tired now,' she said tensely.

'Not at all,' he murmured, standing up and staring down at her. 'We have all our lives in front of us, after all. I'll be in touch. Sweet . . . er . . . dreams, Kirra.'

And he left, swinging his jacket off her hatstand and slinging it over his shoulder carelessly.

Kirra stayed where she was for a long time, then got up and deliberately poured herself a neat brandy which she took back to the settee. Curling up in the corner, she sipped the brandy abstractedly.

'I can no longer not believe this is happening

to me,' she mused. 'I can no longer help but admit there is a sort of fatal fascination, quote-unquote, about him even now.' She stared into space for a long time. 'But there must be some way . . . of getting through to him. Oh God, I *am* tired. Too tired to think straight.'

CHAPTER FIVE

A WEEK later, he was as good as his word.

A reception-room had been hired at the new Gold Coast International Hotel, a cocktail party arranged, the highlight of which was to be the anouncement of a proposed merger between Munro's and Remington Enterprises.

Kirra arrived with her parents, and the photos of her in a stunning little black dress were to feature in Sunday paper social columns. Matt Remington, looking tall and distinguished and not at all remote, met them in the foyer. And he went out of his way from that moment to charm Naomi further, he also worded his speech simply, with no hint of a rescue operation being mounted but as if it were an honour to be associated with Sir Kenneth Munro.

Kirra could not help appreciating her parents' relief, which they were able to hide from all but her, and the fact that her father looked suddenly so much more buoyant. They even managed for the two-hour duration of the cocktail party to stop worrying about her and her broken engagement to Jeremy.

She also took the opportunity to observe Matt Remington in action socially. It wasn't a large crowd but, apart from the top management of Munro's and their wives, there were advertising agency executives, financial and business reporters, also a television crew in the wings, and some legal and banking representatives. And it occurred to Kirra that she'd never seen anyone accorded so much deference as her

father in this kind of milieu, yet her husband-to-be
—the thought made her quiver—certainly generated
it. He also, she noticed, had the sprinkling of
younger women in the crowd either simpering or
glancing at him furtively—apart from one, that was:
an upwardly mobile redhead who greeted him with
poise but a challenging look in her green eyes. When
she met the same redhead in the powder-room and
found herself to be on the receiving end of a
venomous green look, Kirra drew her own conclusions.

The only other incident of interest was when a tall,
excessively thin man in an exaggeratedly tailored suit
with a nipped-in waist and long-tailed jacket came up
to Matt and clapped him on the shoulder.

'Good to see you, old son,' he said jovially. 'Must
be ten . . . fifteen years?'

'At least, Morrie. What are you doing here?' Matt
asked, and, watching him, Kirra was aware of a
subtle change in his expression, a slight narrowing of
his eyes, the faintest hardening of his mouth. She
looked at the other man in some surprise and decided
he had a shifty look about him.

'Earning a quid, Matt, earning a quid. I'm into advertising these days,' Morrie said genially. 'So you're
extending the empire to good old Queensland these
days, eh? Can't say I blame you', he added with a
lascivious look around, letting his eyes linger on
Kirra. 'Always said the birds up here were beaut!'

'Your conversation was never edifying, Morrie,'
Matt replied with the coldest, most cutting look Kirra
had ever seen, and he turned away deliberately.

Morrie shrugged and drifted over to the bar.

But of course the *coup de grâce* to the evening
came when the party was starting to break up and

Matt said to her parents, 'I've persuaded Kirra to have dinner with me tonight. Would you mind very much if we slipped away now?'

Kirra had schooled herself for this moment, and when her parents turned to her simultaneously, she was able to smile ruefully, and say, 'It's true.'

'Not at all . . .'

'Of course you may . . .'

Sir Kenneth and Lady Munro spoke together, then looked at each other and laughed. 'Off you go,' Naomi said with a wave of her hand. 'We'll take care of the stragglers!'

Matt took Kirra's arm and led her away. She looked back once to see her parents staring at each other with raised eyebrows and identical expressions of bemused speculation that would have been comical in other circumstances.

The restaurant was luxurious and dim, and the *maitre d'* greeted Matt by name; then he recognised Kirra and was virtually bowled over with delight. 'Mr Remington and Miss *Munro*,' he said reverently. 'What a night!'

Matt grinned. 'I hope you've a table away from the limelight for us, Edward.

'Rest assured, I have,' Edward replied. 'Not even your best friends will know you're here, let alone any gossip columnists—if you so wish it.'

'For the time being, anyway—we may dance later.'

Kirra said nothing until the flutter of waiters unfurling cream damask napkins and presenting menus had subsided, and the two cocktails on the house had arrived.

Then she sipped hers and said, 'I still can't understand how I'd never even heard your name before

. . . before . . .'

'Before you ran into me again,' he supplied. 'Hadn't you?'

'No. And then I had to pump a friend for information.'

'Ah. The source of your knowledge about my father, I presume?'

Kirra nodded. 'Her husband is heavily into motor-racing, when he's not trying to design the perfect house. Had you no ambition to follow in your father's footsteps?'

He looked at her across the candle flame, and she noticed the little green flecks in his eyes. 'No.'

Kirra grimaced and stirred her drink with the straw. 'End of subject.'

'My father is not a subject I care to elaborate on,' he said drily. 'But in case you're wondering again, my disenchantment with him began when I was about six. He put my mother through hell and periodically dragged me around the race-tracks of the world with a gaggle of gorgeous girls in attendance.'

'And hangers-on like Morrie,' Kirra said quietly.

His hazel eyes narrowed, then after a moment he said, 'That was rather acute of you, Kirra.'

She shrugged. 'There was also a red-headed PR or something lady there tonight, with green eyes and, should we say, prior knowledge of you. I had this thought,' she went on as it was his turn to grimace, but with a glint of amusement, 'it crossed my mind to wonder, in fact, how often I would be bumping into . . . ladies like that.'

'So you could check them off a list?'

'So I could be prepared,' she said blandly. 'After all, you did quote the King of Siam to me, but I too know the musical version almost word for word, and the context of your quote I happen to know every word of. How does it go?' she said reflectively. ' "A girl must be like a blossom, with honey for just one bee . . . a man must live like a honey-bee and gather all he can . . . To fly from blossom to blossom, a honey-bee must be free. A blossom must not ever fly from bee . . . to bee . . . to bee," ' she finished gently. 'Is that how our marriage will be? Oh, I forgot the bit about the human male being pleased by many women, but the bee analogy says it all, really.'

His eyes never left her face, and she thought she detected a glint of admiration in them this time, which he confirmed, although making her want to hit him, by saying appreciatively, 'You're in good form tonight, Kirra. I'm glad we'll be able to stimulate each other mentally.'

'You haven't answered the question,' she said with irony.

'I suppose,' he said thoughtfully, 'that depends on the state of our marriage and how fulfilling it is. I may . . . er . . . have some faults, but I'm generally happy with one woman at a time, so the honey-bee syndrome doesn't altogether fit, wouldn't you say?'

'Perhaps,' she conceded, with a mocking little smile, 'if it's as you say. What I'm really trying to get at is, if the state of our marriage should become . . . unfulfilling in your estimation, and you decided you were justified in being unfaithful to me—even one woman at a time—would I be allowed the same privilege?'

He raised an eyebrow. 'Would you want it? It seems to go against your theories on love.'

Kirra laughed softly. 'I thought so. Had you considered that you might be more like your playboy father than you thought?'

In the silence that followed, Kirra knew she had hit home, had at last found a weak spot in Matthew Remington's defences, because for a second the world seemed to stand still as their eyes clashed, and it was her turn to receive that cool, cutting look, to see again that hardening of his mouth before he deliberately looked away. When he looked back, his hazel eyes were clear, but something in them made her shiver inwardly. A sort of enigmatic intensity that somehow made her think she was going to suffer a reprisal for her remark. She was to discover later that she was not wrong.

For the meantime, however, he said, 'We'll have to wait and see, won't we? I'm fairly certain it will be quite some time before you, at least, consider taking a legion of lovers.'

Kirra nipped her straw so sharply she thought she'd bitten it through. 'You've mentioned that before,' she murmured, keeping her temper with difficulty. 'You assumptions about women are quite nauseating, you know.'

'Are they?'

'*Yes*. We're not *all* pure sensualists, as you are, you know.'

'No?' he said idly.

'No,' she replied flatly. 'It takes a bit more than the old barefoot, pregnant and tied-to-the-kitchen-sink approach nowadays—and before you pick me up on the barefoot and tied-to-the-kitchen-sink bit, I'm sure one can feel equally imprisoned in the kind of luxury you no doubt have in mind.'

'Like a prisoner in a gilded cage. Have you quite finished, Kirra?'

She glared at him.

'Because I think you've done your avowed intention

of fighting me proud tonight. Have a break. Your digestive juices might appreciate it.'

What she might have replied was never uttered, as the first course was served. She'd ordered smoked salmon, and as she stared at it, atop a round crisp half of a lettuce by the look at it, complete with chives and thin, trimmed wedges of toast, she thought—temper, temper, Kirra! Don't be a fool, it will get you nowhere . . .

She picked up her knife and fork and sighed inwardly. The thing is, she mused, I still find it hard to believe this is not a nightmare I'm going to wake up from soon.

'All right,' she said. 'You choose something to talk about.'

He smiled faintly. 'Let's see—black becomes you. It makes your skin look . . . tantalisingly translucent.'

'Thank you.'

'Are you doing anything this weekend?'

'I . . . no.'

'I don't remember if I mentioned to you that I have a place on the Tweed.'

'You did.'

'Would you care to come down this weekend and see it?'

'Do I have a choice?'

'*We* . . . have a deal, Kirra,' he reminded her.

'Of course—how foolish of me to forget. Yes, I'll come.' She looked at him briefly, her eyes suddenly shadowed and strained, her face pale, and she put her knife and fork down with her smoked salmon only half eaten. 'I . . . I'm sorry but . . . you're right about my digestive juices. They seem to be tied in a knot if that's possible—well, something seems to be.'

Matt signalled the waiter, who removed their

plates, and he murmured something to him about delaying their main course, then looked at her. 'Have some wine,' he ordered.

She did, and by the time she had sipped half a glass some colour had returned to her cheeks. 'Sorry,' she said then. 'I'm fine now.'

But, although she managed to eat most of her main meal, and even follow his lead again conversation-wise, perhaps he saw the effort it was, because he didn't attempt to linger once they'd had their coffee, nor did he suggest they dance, although the band had struck up.

If Edward was disappointed at their early departure, he gave no sign, and bowed them out as if they were royalty.

Kirra couldn't help breathing a sigh of relief as the blue Rolls headed towards Main Beach, but her relief was to be short-lived when Matt parked it, got out and came round to help her out, and she knew he intended coming up to the apartment with her.

She thought of saying something, but could formulate nothing that didn't sound childishly petulant. She also felt exhausted and incredibly tense.

He took her key from her and opened the door, then stood back for her to enter. She hesitated briefly, then walked into the lounge, flicking on a lamp that shed a pool of soft pink light, and she dropped her bag on to the glass-topped table and said huskily the only thing she seemed capable of saying, 'What now?'

He came over to her and took her chin in his hand. 'What now?' he repeated, barely audibly, his eyes searching her face and his fingers roaming her jawline, the line of her cheek and throat. 'I think, as your prospective husband, it's my duty to try to relax you, Kirra. Like this . . .'

She made a stunned sound of protest, but he ignored it and she moved convulsively at what she saw in his eyes—a naked look of desire that made her skin shiver. And she knew suddenly that to fight him would be useless, that he would overwhelm her with ease, and tonight take pleasure in his victory—that this was to be his reprisal.

But there must be *some* way to resist this, Kirra, she told herself dazedly, as he drew her into his arms and slid one hand up her back to the nape of her neck beneath the heavy fall of her hair. I refuse to be treated like this . . .

She discovered not much later that her sentiments were like wishes on the wind against the almost mesmerising power he chose to exert over her. He didn't attempt to kiss her immediately, but his long fingers on the nape of her neck, stroking gently, unwittingly released a knot of tension; together with her awful confusion, and gradually reduced her to an almost trance-like state. But at the same time she was oddly conscious of how her body was resting against his, how her thighs felt against his and how her breasts were cushioned against his chest, how from straining every muscle to turn her body into a brick wall of resistance, she was achieving the opposite.

Oh God, I keep forgetting about this . . . how could I? I mustn't give way to it . . .

Perhaps her tortured thoughts were mirrored in her eyes, because he smiled slightly, a faint, cool movement of his lips before he bent his head and teased her lips apart.

It was a kiss she could not end, could only accept as if drugged with the feel and taste of him, her memories of the first time he had kissed her coming alive beneath his hands and mouth. How right she felt in his arms when he kissed her this way . . .

But if there was a spark of hope in her eyes, a supplication in the set of her parted, trembling lips when he lifted his head, he chose to douse it cruelly. 'Do you see now that you sometimes talk a lot of nonsense, Kirra?' he murmured, scanning the pale oval of her face beneath half-lowered eyelids.

She closed her eyes, and for a moment could only bury her face in his shoulder against the faintly rough surface of his charcoal jacket as she tried desperately to think. 'Yes,' she whispered desolately at last, and lifted her eyes to his to see that his face above his white shirt and dark green and black striped tie was set in harsh, uncompromising lines. She also discovered she felt curiously naked in her sleeveless black dress, and realised she was clutching the front of his beautiful tailored jacket like a hot-handed schoolgirl.

She opened her hand and put the back of it to her mouth. 'I . . . yes.' It came out muffled and sounded supremely vulnerable, and she cleared her throat and staggered slightly as he released her abruptly.

'Goodnight, then. I'll pick you up at ten o'clock on Saturday morning,' he said briefly. 'We can resume our love-hate relationship then.'

Kirra watched him go, then stumbled into her bedroom and sat down on her bed, gripping her hands together tightly and biting her lip hard enough to draw blood. For it had finally come home to her that Matthew Remington was not only disillusioned and very dangerous, but that he was also going to marry her come hell or high water.

The drive from Surfers' Paradise to Tweed Heads is

unexciting. The beaches that collectively make up the City of the Gold Coast are not really visible from the Pacific Highway, there are busy shopping centres all the way down it and usually plenty of traffic. Kirra had also driven the tedious length of it more times than she cared to remember.

She had never been driven down it in a magnificent late-model, dark blue Rolls-Royce coupé with cream leather trim, with the hood down, which distinguished the trip somewhat, she had to admit, although not favourably, and she thought once, I wonder where he keeps his battered Land Rover?

Apart from this, she also had her frayed nerves to deal with, for they had not stood the test of the intervening days well. In fact, it had taken a supreme effort of will not to do either of two things—confess to her parents the predicament she was in, or flee the country. Nor had her nerves been helped by the sight of her tormentor at precisely ten o'clock on this beautiful Saturday morning, standing outside her front door in jeans and a white cotton-knit shirt, looking freshly showered and shaved, but oddly lazy about those hazel eyes, as if he hadn't been up long.

Which he hadn't, he told her. He'd only arrived home from a business trip to Melbourne very late the previous evening and had slept in.

Kirra, who had been awake before dawn herself, had glinted him a taut, unsympathetic look. She'd also been mostly silent on the drive down, particularly after a verbal skirmish concerning his Rolls.

Because of the roof being down and the traffic which had frequently held them up, she had felt highly conspicuous, which had prompted her to say at yet another red light where people all around were craning their heads to look at them, 'Dad reckons these kind of cars are more trouble than they're worth. People enjoy scratching them and trying to steal the insignia, and they're also insanely expensive in Australia, and only a status symbol.'

'He's probably right,' Matt replied tranquilly. 'But I don't own racehorses or yachts, I don't go in for vast country or town mansions—as yet. I don't have expensive mistresses stashed about, I don't have my own plane, so I figured I could afford to shout myself one. The other thing is that they are an investment in that they hold their value better than most other cars, and you can't deny that, as a status symbol, they have a kind of class.'

'I hesitate to say this, but since you mentioned class again, do you see me as a status symbol or an investment? Or both?'

He considered. 'Both, I would say. I also think you're looking gorgeously windblown, which is an important consideration with this kind of car—a girl in a dowdy headscarf can spoil the image.'

Kirra ground her teeth secretly—one deal she had made with herself in the turmoil of the past few days was not to rise to the bait so readily, yet here she was, breaking that rule so soon. I shall play dumb for a while, she vowed.

But that didn't seem to faze him, either. He drove with almost negligent ease, seemingly totally oblivious of the quiet furore their progress was creating, but once they turned inland from Tweed Heads and left the traffic behind them, he upped the speed and the big car flashed along breathtakingly but with superb suspension.

The Tweed River, together with the Clarence and the Richmond, make up an area of New South Wales known as the Northern Rivers. It is in fact the most northern, and the town of Tweed Heads at its mouth is on the border of Queensland. But, while Tweed Heads is very much a holiday, tourist town, once you leave it behind and head inland, the magic of the river takes over as the road winds along beside its broad, peaceful reaches. It's sugar-cane country on the lower banks of the Tweed, and they turned off the highway before the Condong Sugar Mill, at Tumbulgum, a picturesque little village, and crossed the river by bridge.

It was a steep, winding drive on the other side, which the big car took in its stride, and before long they turned off the road and through a pair of white gateposts.

'Is this it?' Kirra asked, gazing around.

'Like it?' The car came to a stop beside what she first thought was a very old farmhouse. But it was the view and position that held her spellbound for a time.

'Oh,' she said, very softly. They were atop a foothill, a curved, grassy dome that swept smoothly down to the river, a hill that afforded a view upstream to the town of Murwillumbah, itself clinging to the foothills of Mount Warning, a hill with the backdrop of the Lamington Range which, in the clear air, was tinted mysteriously purple. A hill with a view downstream, of the river broadening between patchwork canefields. His very own hill, by the look of it.

She turned to him at last. 'It's incredible.'

'Glad you think so.'

Something in his voice made Kirra narrow her eyes, something different, and it stirred a chord within her, but she couldn't put her finger on it. She turned her attention to the house and gasped as she realised it wasn't old at all, just built to look it out of red cedar which had weathered to a silvery grey. It was also more of a cottage, two-storeyed with a steep roof, dormer windows, a couple of tall stone chimneys and a veranda around three sides. There was a stone terrace below the front veranda with a brick barbecue, no formal garden but a flat area of lawn upon which several colourful chickens were picking unperturbed.

Behind the house there were some outbuildings beneath a clump of huge gumtrees: a garage, stables and what looked like a studio, with wide windows and a skylight.

'Do you paint?' she asked as he got out and opened her door for her.

'No.' He followed the direction of her gaze. 'That's where Min lives. She's a sculptress, so I converted an old shed for her. She should be around somewhere.'

'Min?'

'It's short for Minerva—the name her father was thoughtless enough to bestow on her at birth. She lives here, and in return for the studio, looks after the place for me.'

Kirra looked confused and surprised. 'On her own? Doesn't she get lonely?'

'Min likes being by herself from time to time. She won't stay for ever though, and speaking of her —here she is.'

A screen door on the veranda opened and out came a tall, attractive woman with very short, dark hair. As she got closer, Kirra saw that she was probably in her thirties, with a lithe figure fairly exposed in sky-blue shorts and a pink shirt tied to reveal her slender midriff, and intelligent, deep blue eyes—and a curl of suspicion awoke in Kirra's mind.

Then Matt was introducing them, and Kirra received a sweeping look from head to toe before Min said warmly, 'Welcome, Kirra. Matt was right—you're beautiful!'

Kirra blushed brightly, and could only murmur 'How do you do?' in return.

But if Min noticed her discomfort she only went on to say briskly that she'd set out lunch for them, that she'd done all the preparations for a barbecue for dinner if that was all right with Matt, and if there was anything Kirra needed, just to give her a call.

'Won't you join us for the barbecue?' Matt asked.

'Not tonight,' Min said decisively.'I'm consumed with inspiration at the moment. But if you still want company for lunch tomorrow, I'll be around.' And walked away slowly towards the studio with a friendly wave.

'Min never changes,' Matt said with a grin. 'Care to come in?'

Kirra said she would.

He carried their bags in at the same time, and again Kirra was impressed—it was lovely inside. The walls were panelled with cedar, but this time a warm honey colour, and the floor was the same, although sealed and shining. Downstairs consisted of only three rooms: an open-plan lounge, dining and kitchen area about a turned, three-stage, timber staircase, a bedroom and a bathroom. But there was a warm, old-world charm to it, a comfortable sofa and deep chairs in front of an enormous stone fireplace, a long refectory table with some old, bentwood chairs, and the kitchen nook had copper pots hanging from hooks and an old-fashioned dresser for china. The bedroom wasn't large, but it had its own fireplace, a brass bedstead and a chintz spread.

Upstairs was even more fascinating, a loft really, just one large room with embrasures and window-seats around the dormer windows, a soaring ceiling with rafters, and it was furnished as a bedroom-cum-study.

'What a marvellous retreat,' she heard herself saying sincerely as they came downstairs again.

'Thanks,' he drawled. 'Coming from you, that's high praise, I'm sure.'

'I meant it,' Kirra said stiffly. Then, as he raised his eyebrows quizzically, she added, 'All right—but I did.'

'Am I to take it,' he was standing on the step above her, looking down at her amusedly, 'that your ill-humour of earlier has disappeared?'

She ran her forefinger along the banister, bending her head so that her hair hid her face, and said quietly, 'I wouldn't take anything for granted about me if I were you—*I* certainly won't be, because you see I'm just concentrating on getting on from moment to moment.'

'Yes, ma'am,' he said ruefully as she lifted her head and sent him a steady, blue-grey glance. 'Shall we have lunch? I don't know about you, but I'm starving.'

The lunch Min had set out was perfect for a hot day. Slices of rare cold beef with horseradish sauce, cold pork with mango chutney—Munro's, Kirra noted—tender, fresh asparagus, beetroot, tomatoes, hard-boiled eggs, warm, crusty rolls, and to finish, a bowl piled high with apples, oranges and grapes. Matt made tea for them.

Then he said, 'Why don't you slip a swimsuit under your jeans—do you ride, by the way?'

Kirra nodded.

'Would you like to ride down to the river for a swim?'

Kirra nodded again. 'But I'll clear up here first.'

'Min will probably appreciate that if she's creating. I'll change and get the horses ready.'

She heard him moving about above her as she cleared away quickly and competently. Then she went into the downstairs bedroom, where he'd put her bag, and closed the door.

She unpacked a few things and changed absently into her rose-pink swimsuit, put her jeans back on, tied her hair back—all the while deep in thought.

The implications of this weekend had been obvious, she had thought. By fair means or foul, she would end up in Matt Remington's bed . . .

'What do you mean—fair means or foul,' she asked herself beneath her breath. '*All* his means are . . . conniving to say the least, but I've got the feeling that *this* weekend the steel fist will be invisible beneath the proverbial velvet glove, and that, dear Kirra, is doubly dangerous.' She closed her eyes briefly, and then found herself wondering about Min. Surely he wouldn't . . .?

It was the sound of a horse harumphing outside and the jingle of bits that brought her out of her reverie.

'This is heavenly,' Kirra said idly as she chewed a stalk of juicy grass.

The swim had been refreshing and the ride very pleasant, not only because of the scenery but also because of her mount, a beautifully mannered and mouthed chestnut mare called Dandelion.

'Oh, isn't she pretty!' she had been moved to remark on first sight.

Matt had nodded non-committally and helped her into the saddle. He'd also kept a very close eye on her from his tall brown gelding with three white feet for the first few minutes, and ridden close enough to be able to grab the mare's bridle.

Finally Kirra had said indignantly, 'You don't have to *hover* like that. I told you I could ride, and anyway, anyone could ride her on a piece of cotton!'

'Anyone could not,' he had said. 'She responds to bad riding and heavy hands like the temperamental female of the species she is. But you'll do,' he'd added, and had moved away to take the lead down the path.

Kirra had murmured to Dandelion that she didn't believe a word of it, and weren't *males* of the species unbearable sometimes? Then the pleasure of the ride had taken over. And now she was lying on her towel, unable not to enjoy the sunlit afternoon, the smell of grass, the birdsong and the quiet murmur of the river. I must be mad, she reflected. I'm about to enter the most dangerous, unknown period of my life, I can come up with no plan of action which any strategist from Hannibal to my own father would not warn me is the height of folly . . . but I'm enjoying the birds and the bees, talking of which . . .

She sat up and squinted over to where Matt was sitting on his towel with his arms resting on his knees, staring across the water. His hair was damp and lying across his forehead, and his streamlined body still glistened with droplets of water, and she said abruptly, 'Are you expecting me to sleep with you tonight?'

He drew his gaze from the river to her, leisurely, and answered her question with another. 'Would you like to?'

'No . . . I . . . if it's a question of choice, no, I would rather not.'

'It's certainly not a question of rape,' he said wryly, 'if that's what you had on your mind.'

She laughed shortly. 'Not rape . . . perhaps seduction,' she suggested, plucking another stem of grass. 'And perhaps I should warn you I don't have a great reputation . . . in bed.'

He raised his eyebrows. 'It takes two to tango, Kirra,' he murmured, 'if you'll forgive the triteness. At whose hands was this reputation created, may I ask? Or perhaps I can guess,' he said softly. 'Fiancé number one.'

Kirra pressed her lips together as Matt regarded her steadily for a moment, then leant on his elbow and said casually, 'I normally don't believe in prying into what . . . has gone before, but I think you had better tell me about him. It . . . er . . . appears to me that a lot of what has followed might stem from him. He obviously conned you into believing he loved you for yourself, not your parents' wealth. Is that right?'

Kirra parted her lips, then took refuge in flippancy. 'Spot on! Bravo! In retrospect, he was one of those idle men, heavily into sporting achievements, but without the wherewithal to support his expensive tastes. He was also good-looking, fun to be with and very adept at hiding the fact that he was on the make. Women pursued him and . . . my heart used to go bang, bang, bang, whenever he was near. He assured me I had the same effect on him.' she said drily, and added, barely audibly, 'I shouldn't have been let out, I was so naïve.'

'How old?' he asked.

She grimaced. 'Nineteen.'

'And what burst the bubble?'

'I overheard him one day. He was talking to a friend of his, and it was only one those amazing co-incidences that I happened to be within earshot without his knowing. He . . . they were discussing me in . . . intimate detail.' She broke off and shivered. 'I gathered that I wasn't quite up to his standards in certain respects, but that I might just improve with experience. He laughed, and said that nobody could accuse me of being sophisticated or imaginative in bed, and that he might have to get that kind of fun elsewhere after we were married, but until we were, he was being very careful. It was, after all, he said, a minor consideration compared to all the lovely loot I represented and the fact that my parents doted on me, etc, etc!'

'Oh, dear . . .'

'There was more,' Kirra said bleakly, conscious of a fatalistic determination to tell him the lot now she had started. 'He also said he doubted if he was built to be faithful to any one woman, and it was fortunate that while I might not satisfy him, there was no doubt I thought the sun shone out of him, and if he could keep it that way, there was no reason he could see why I should interfere with his ability with women, the ability to lay them in the aisles begging for more.'

There was a short silence, then Matt said, 'What did you do? Break it off there and then?'

'No, I was . . . speechless. I couldn't believe not only what I'd been hearing, but the . . . coldness it represented. I was just stunned at how adroit he'd been and completely mortified at how right my parents had been about him. Although he charmed most people he met, he hadn't altogether fooled them. I . . . went home and planned to write him a letter ending it all so that I wouldn't have to see him again, but the next day he was killed in a water-skiing accident. For a moment, when I heard the news, I wondered if I'd wished it on him, and then there was the problem of everyone assuming I was heart-broken, when I was actually—well horrified but . . .'

'I know what you mean.'

'Do you?'

'Yes—it's pointless and tasteless to speak ill of the dead, so you had to accept all the sympathy and feel an utter fraud. Didn't you tell anyone?'

'Only my parents initially, then my best friend Pippa, and finally, Jeremy, that's all. He'd known Bret actually, and disliked him. He . . .' She stopped and sighed.

'Go on—tell me about Jeremy,' Matt prompted. 'For one reason, if no other—I'd like remove any stigma attached to my name in your mind concerning Jeremy. Do you think you would ever have married him?'

Kirra stirred restlessly. 'I don't know,' she said honestly. 'Because he *was* one of the few of us not to be taken in by Bret—he even tried to warn me once but I wouldn't be warned—because he understood, I suppose I . . . gravitated towards him because of that.' She shrugged. 'And he was so nice and so sure he loved me and so patient.' She grimaced.

'The antithesis of Bret.'

'I suppose so,' Kirra conceded.

'But instead of admitting that to yourself, you kept coming up with delays—you were delaying the wedding in your mind when you met me, weren't you, Kirra?'

Kirra looked across the water. 'Oh . . . yes!' She turned back, her eyes suddenly glinting fiercely. 'I

was also wondering if I should inflict myself on him,
for what it's worth. Can you not understand at all
why . . . I was so mixed up?'

Matt sat up and frowned faintly. 'At nineteen—I
guess we all go through some form of trauma or
another with the opposite sex, but you're twenty-
two, Kirra, a big girl now. You can probably look
back on other follies you committed in your late
teens, on the fact that you assumed you knew
everything in those days . . . and laugh at yourself
now. Why carry this chip on your shoulder?'

Kirra stared at him with a set mouth, then
murmured, 'You're the last person I should be discussing this with.'

'On the contrary, the best, as things stand. And on
the subject of how good you are in bed,' he said
softly, 'why let the immature crowings of a two-bit
louse influence you in your opinion of yourself?'

Kirra opened her mouth to reply tartly, but there
was something completely unanswerable about his
logic, no way to explain what a vulnerable area it was
whether you were nineteen or thirty-nine, she
suspected. So she said tautly, in an oblique cross-
thrust, 'Tell me about Min.'

A smile twisted his lips. 'I've known Min for . . .
let's see, sixteen or seventeen years now.'

'An old friend,' Kirra said ironically.

He held her gaze, then said deliberately, 'She was
more than that—for a time.'

Kirra's lips parted. 'You . . . do you mean . . .?'

He nodded. 'It was also quite a long time ago, and
we were able to remain friends when it ended.'

'Why are you telling me this?' she whispered, her
eyes stunned.

He looked amused. 'You did ask me. Besides, it's

only what you suspected, isn't it?'

'All the same . . .'

He laughed at her openly. 'Anyway, you've just told me all your secrets, and as you've met her now, it's better that you *do* know, so there can be no mis-understandings in the future. I'm sure you'll find you'll like her. She's very kind and very sane.'

'I can't imagine why you didn't marry her, then,' Kirra broke in bitterly. 'I really not only hate you, but despise you s-sometimes!' Her voice shook and she jumped up tensely and ran down to the river, but he caught her and pulled her into his arms at the edge of the water.

'Still fighting?' he said softly, his eyes flickering from her mutinously set mouth down to her breasts beneath the rose-pink lycra.

'If you dare,' she said through her teeth, 'to try to kiss me after . . . in almost the same breath as parading your former love-life in front of me, I'll . . .'

'Jealous?' he broke in, his eyes gleaming with devilry. 'You needn't be. It's been over and dead for a long time.'

'No!' Her lips stayed parted in horror at the very thought. Then she said scathingly, 'That's like expecting me to believe you were jealous of Jeremy!'

'Oh, if you'd married him, I would have been.'

Her eyes widened disbelievingly.

'Kirra,' he said, as one would to a backward child, 'I'd have to be totally unmoved by you to have been jealous—which I'm not. There's be no point in marrying you if I were.'

'Not totally? How fortunate,' she murmured mockingly.

He grinned. 'Perhaps I could have put it better

—like this, for example.'

She tried to struggle out of his arms, but she slipped and they fell into the shallows, sending a spray of water arcing above them, and all she achieved was to be still in his arms, half submereged in the river with her skin fresh and satiny beneath his hands, her hair dark and streaming, and his mouth on hers . . .

When it ended, he picked her up and carried her out of the water, she was breathing erratically as he put her down on her feet and steadied her with his hands about her waist.

'Still hate me?' he asked.

Her eyes were dark and tormented. 'I . . .'

'I don't really mind what you call it—for the time being, that is.' He smoothed the wet hair off her face. 'Shall we,' he paused as she tensed, 'ride some more? Dandelion's getting restless.'

They rode the boundaries of the property, then washed the horses down together and stabled them for the night with their feeds. There was no sign of Min, but Kirra did see the elderly Land Rover parked in the shed.

'Your father's right,' Matt said as he noticed her staring at it. 'I keep that because there are times when the Rolls is a nuisance.'

Kirra grimaced. 'I have to be honest—Dad would probably love one, but Mum's not a very good driver, although she can't see it herself. Oh, she's all right in traffic, it's stationary things she has trouble with, like garage walls, fences and trees.'

Matt laughed. 'I like your mother.'

'She certainly likes you,' Kirra said quietly, staring again at the Land Rover, then she turned to him.

'Will you tell me one thing? What *were* you doing at Yamba? Do you do that kind of thing often?'

'I . . .' He stopped. 'Should we shower and change first? And I'll get the fire going for the barbecue . . .'

'You're not going to tell me, are you?' she broke in. 'That's not fair.'

'It's no deep dark secret, and yes, I will try to explain my . . . occasional bouts of wanderlust to you, Kirra,' he said. 'Over our meal, though. Coming?'

'I . . . yes.'

CHAPTER SIX

KIRRA put on a loose grey dress printed with yellow and white daises after she had showered, then tied back her hair with a grey ribbon and slid her feet into yellow sandals.

She'd smoothed body lotion all over her skin, but other than that she'd used no cosmetics. Just the basic me, she thought.

There was music playing, and she recognised the stately but lilting *Rondo* from Mozart's 'Horn Concerto', which soothed her mental turmoil for a time. But when it finished there was silence, and no reason for her to delay leaving the sanctuary of the downstairs bedroom.

She stayed for a few minutes longer though, deep in thought because there were some things that were becoming increasingly hard to explain . . . such as how she could enjoy being kissed by a man who admired her body but not much else about her, or he wouldn't be bargaining with her as if she were a desirable chattel.

What's more, she thought, he has me in the most incredible corner and I can think of no way out, bar locking myself in here until he promises to take me home . . . A hunger-strike! Why didn't I think of that? And why, she smiled grimly, do I have the feeling he'd work his way round that one, too?

A knock on the door interrupted her thoughts, and she jumped, then called, 'Come in.'

He didn't come in, just opened the door and

started to say something, then stopped and frowned faintly.

As for Kirra, she was unable to tear her eyes away from him; he had showered and now wore jeans and a blue and white striped shirt, with his hair still damp.

'What's the matter?' he said abruptly.

She coloured and switched her gaze away angrily —in fact, that was what she reminded herself of, an angry cat flicking its tail. 'Nothing—I'm just fine,' she said sardonically.

He strolled into the room and paused to look at her searchingly. 'If you could relax, we might be able to make some progress.'

'Towards what? On second thoughts, don't tell me, I can guess.' She returned his look ironically.

'Towards being really good together—again. And I mean companion-wise.'

'Matt,' she said deliberately, 'I must warn you that, contrary to what my past history might have indicated, I'm no good at playing games.'

'Are we playing games?' he asked quietly.

'Yes. Cat-and-mouse games, and I'm the mouse.' She broke off and had to grimace ruefully, and mutter exasperatedly, 'I wish you'd make up your mind, Kirra!'

He looked at her quizzically, but she recovered quickly.

'The simple fact is that you're forcing me to marry you. You're also using your considerable experience and expertise with women quite deliberately and shamefully to play upon the fact that I once responded to you physically and in my book, *Mr Remington*,' she said scornfully, 'that makes you no better than Bret, although I suppose to call you a two-bit louse on the make would be inaccurate—a two-million-bit louse might be more appropriate.'

'Bravo, Kirra!' he said, his eyes glinting wickedly. 'This . . . cad of the first water stands utterly reproved. You're also quite sensational when you're angry, you know.'

'Oh . . . why didn't I just lock myself in?' she asked despairingly.

'Now that would have been childish,' he replied 'and I prefer you when you're firing straight from the hip. You'll feel better after you've had something to eat. It's beautiful outside and the fire's going well.'

He barbecued chops and sausages, and they ate them with the salads from lunch time plus a dish of ratatouille Min had made and left to be heated up. There was also a strawberry shortcake with ice-cream to follow, and he opened a bottle of wine.

It was unbelievably peaceful on Matt Remington's private hilltop, and as Kirra sipped her wine she watched the pale smoke of the fire swirling against the dark of the sky. There seemed to be a million stars out, and a prim little new moon descending in the west.

'Tell me about this wanderlust of yours,' she said at last.

He shrugged slightly. 'I think it stems from when I was a kid and I used to read Rider Haggard, Kipling, *Jock of the Bushveld*, *Memories of a Game Ranger* and later Robert Ruark—I used to dream about the Plains of Serengeti, the Mountains of the Moon . . . places like Etosha Pan and the Kruger National Park. It was my greatest ambition to be a big-game hunter or a game ranger,' he said wryly.

Kirra blinked and thought that if he had told her it had been a serious ambition with him to be a circus clown she would not have been more surprised.

'An odd amibiton for an Australian boy,' she said.

'My mother was South African.'

Kirra stared at him, wide-eyed. 'Tell me about her.'

'She met my father at Kia Lami—that's their grand-prix circuit outside Johannesburg—and was duly dazzled, although she did succeed in marrying him. Possibly because she had a lot of very large and moral male relatives,' he said drily, and added, 'She was a farmer's daughter and always stayed one at heart—I don't mean she was uncultured, but she was capable, loyal, stubborn, tremendously family-orientated and she had an affinity with the earth and growing things. And she paid dearly for the one mistake of her life.'

'Did she pine for South Africa?'

'Yes, but it wasn't only that. They were completely mismatched. All her qualities represented one thing to my father—being tied down. Oddly enough, and I think this was the one thing that made life a little bearable for her, she was a lot like the Remingtons and they liked and admired her. They're also a capable, cautious bunch . . . until Dad came along.'

'She also had you,' Kirra said quietly. 'Did she take you back to South Africa?'

'Every few years. I loved it, and my uncle, one of her brothers, was a game ranger with the Transvaal Nature Conservation Division.'

'How come your mother didn't divorce your father, if it was as you say?'

'She was very proud, perhaps too proud to admit the failure of her marriage, and anyway, he swore he'd never part with me. I couldn't understand it while I was growing up—it was pretty obvious whose side I was on, but I did work it out eventually. We,

she and I, were his one link with the Remingtons
. . . the rest of the family. If it hadn't been for us,
they'd have washed their hands of him a lot sooner.'

Kirra shivered. 'No wonder you're . . . so cynical.'

He glanced at her, then grinned. 'Actually, I'm a
lot less cynical about it since I've restored the family
fortune, our branch of it. And,' he sobered, 'for
what it's worth, my father and the former supposed
love of my life are still together, and to all intents and
purposes, quietly happy.'

Kirra stirred. 'She must—you said she was older
than you, but she must be a lot younger than he is.'

'Over twenty years, but for all that, she seems to
have reformed him. It's strange what works for some
people.'

'And you,' Kirra said, 'go on safari from time to
time in memory of your mother.'

'Something like that,' he agreed. 'Yes.'

Kirra watched him in silence for a while. He was
looking away from her, staring into the darkness with
the firelight flickering on his face and highlighting the
remoteness of his expression, the lines beside his
mouth, and she thought back to Lover's Point and
remembered how his smile had captured her heart, a
smile she hadn't really seen since. And as she studied
the way his fair hair fell, the set of his mouth, she felt
her heart contract and she was filled with a desire to
bring him back from wherever his mind was wander-
ing.

'I don't know much about South Africa, apart
from the obvious, but after I saw the movie *Out of
Africa*, I read the book and it was just fascinating.
Not only because of Africa, but the way she wrote.
The images she created sort of leapt off the page,
they were so real.'

He looked at her at last. 'If you liked that, you'd have liked my mother. That's the kind of life she'd have loved.'

'Would you . . . no.' Kirra stopped.

'Go on.'

'It just occurred to me,' Kirra said slowly, 'that perhaps you—and your father until he got reformed, have a bit of Denys Finch-Hatton in you.'

It was strange, she reflected later, since it had been in her thoughts only minutes before—that heart-stopping smile that crinkled the corners of his eyes—and to see it again left her feeling oddly breathless.

'Perhaps,' he said. 'I did sometimes wonder if it was the elusiveness about my father that bound my mother to him against her will. I mean, if she'd been able to pin him down, she might also have been able to let him go. That sounds crazy, but . . .'

'I know what you mean. I'm sure it happens,' she said and found herself feeling curiously cold as if from an elusive premonition.

But in fact the breeze had strengthened and the fire was dying down. She sighed inwardly and said quietly, 'I'll clear up.'

'I'll help you.'

They did it in no time at all between them, and as he started the dishwasher, which ran almost soundlessly, Kirra stood in the middle of the kitchen, wondering what to do next.

Matt straightened and glanced at her, then said abruptly, 'Bed for you, I think.'

'Thank you, I enjoyed that,' she said uncertainly.

'Goodnight. Will you be able to sleep?'

'Yes.' He was standing close enough for her to see the green flecks in his eyes, and she thought with a tremor, he'll kiss me and I'll feel like a . . . a foolish, star-struck girl.

He didn't. He studied her meditatively, the cotton dress with its brave yellow and white daisies, the ribbon in her hair, her shadowed eyes. He did put out a hand to touch her hair, but it was almost an absent-minded gesture as he said, 'Off you go, then.'

It was a long time before she got to sleep. Not only were the bed and the house alien, the small sounds different, the lack of noise compared to where she lived almost a noise in itself, but there were her alien thoughts to deal with. Such as why, instead of feeling she had been let off the hook, she should be feeling something different.

It was a blue and gold Sunday morning and they rode after breakfast, higher into the hills where the air was almost intoxicatingly pure and fresh, and alive with the smell of grass-seed and earth.

He made no comment about the faint blue shadows beneath her eyes, and she avoided mentioning anything that wasn't mundane.

But when they found a small pool in a tree-rimmed hollow and dismounted to rest the horses and give them a drink, she leant back against a gumtree, listening to the hum of insects and waving her hat to cool her face—and said unthinkingly, 'It's so beautiful here. If I lived here, I might never want to leave.'

'You wouldn't have to if that's the way you feel.'

She sighed inwardly and thought, I walked into that one . . . why not take it a step further? 'You wouldn't be able to spend much time here.'

He'd been tying the horses to a tree, and he came over and sprawled on the grass at her feet, pushed a hand through his hair and squinted up at her quizzically. 'That would be a problem wherever we lived, but naturally with a wife—and children eventually —I'd try to cut down my travelling as much as possible. Or you might like to come with me as much as possible—there are advantages about having one special place to come home to.'

Kirra stirred. 'Yes,' she said absently.

'We could always extend the house for kids.'

She was silent.

'Do you have anything against kids, Kirra?' he asked at length.

'No. I've never had much to do with children.' She looked down and encountered a searching hazel gaze which told her he knew she was simply going along with this conversation, and she looked away again. Did he *really* expect . . .

'I wouldn't expect you to rush into having a team of babies, Kirra,' he said deliberately.

'You know what you remind me of?' she said. 'That old adage about water wearing away a stone. Perhaps it's an old Afrikaans adage.'

He sat up and said with a faint smile twisting his lips, 'Come down to my level for a while.' He held out his hand.

She took it after a moment and slid down the trunk.

'You didn't sleep well after all, did you?' he said softly.

'No.'

'Do you know what I think?' His hazel gaze was curiously brilliant, and he raised a hand and touched the line of her throat, then let it rest on her chest, his fingers curled lightly about her neck. 'I think there's one way we understand each other perfectly, Kirra, and it's foolish to fight it.'

Her breath caught in her throat, and she trembled beneath the onslaught of the undoubted physical attraction he held for her. She thought how easy it would be to give way to the feel of his hands and mouth on her body, and she wondered how she would feel in the aftermath of his lovemaking, if that final intimacy—and the images of it flooded her mind—would release her from this torture, or chain her to it for ever.

'All the same, if I have a choice,' she whispered, 'I shall fight it.' And she took his wrist and returned his hand to his lap.

'Even when we're married?' he said, barely audibly.

She closed her eyes. 'I don't know yet. I can't visualise that somehow, but no—it would be foolish, and anyway, I'd be reneging on our deal. I won't do that. But until then, foolish or not, I prefer to fight it.'

'You think you can?'

Kirra opened her eyes but stared at her hands first, then lifted her lashes, uncertain of what she would see—that cold yet casual implacability, mostly masked this weekend? She'd found herself wondering last night if she was fighting herself more than him, until she had thought of his mother, enmeshed on a roundabout of love and pride and pain. And in the depth of the night she had come to one conclusion—that she could no longer afford to be disbelieving and distraught, nor could she allow herself to submit to the sensual hold he had over her without compromising her integrity. If she had to go to the altar of his disillusionment and desire for revenge, if she had to pay for her parents' peace of mind, she would at least do so fighting for the right to express her distrust of his motives.

'I think I have to,' she said, and realised the look in his hazel eyes was curiously critical, if anything. As if, although he was looking at her, he was examining something unseen, maybe even foreign to him.

Then his eyes glinted with familiar irony, and he said softly. 'May the best man win—no,' he added as she tensed expectantly, 'I'm not going to afford you the opportunity to fling my . . . considerable experience and expertise with women, quote-unquote, in my face.'

Kirra had lowered her eyes again, but she looked up and her blue-grey glance was steady but with a glimmer of contempt, causing him to break off and lift an eyebrow consideringly at her, and to say thoughtfully, after a while, 'Why do I get the feeling we have a whole . . . new ball-game going?'

'I told you before—I'm no good at games,' she said evenly. 'Believe it or not, this is for real.'

'Would you care to tell me about this new resolution?' he asked with a faint, dry smile.

'No,' she replied briefly.

'But,' he paused and it was there now, she saw, not so much the implacability but a coolly calculating look in his eyes that still had the power to make her feel nervous, 'you look as if you've come up with a secret weapon, my dear Kirra.'

'Perhaps I have,' she murmured, and wondered if she should tell him that it was a strange affinity she felt for a person she had never known, his mother, that had given her this resolution. 'Perhaps I know a bit more about you now,' she said with a faint shrug.

'Don't underestimate me, Kirra,' he warned quietly. 'Or the effect we have on each other.'

'It's not that; if anything, it's the opposite. That

doesn't mean I have to roll over on to my back and beg you to stroke my belly,' she said.

He looked faintly surprised at her choice of words, then absent-mindedly amused, and finally he said wryly, 'So be it.' And he stood up and gave her his hand to help her to her feet.

She took it with no fuss, and he didn't attempt to press any further attentions on her, although when he took the red bandanna he wore round his neck off and dipped it in the pool, he offered it her first.

She splashed her face, bathed her wrists and handed it back, and then they mounted and rode back to the house in silence. But Kirra found herself wondering if all she had achieved was to add fuel to the challenge.

Min was there like a genie, and she came out to greet them with a wave and a grin. 'Hope you're hungry, you two! I've made a traditional Sunday roast dinner.'

Kirra had a quick wash and brush-up, and they sat down to roast lamb with mint sauce, baked potatoes, fresh peas and carrots and a passion-fruit cheesecake to follow.

Fortunately, Min was in an ebullient, talkative mood—the result, she told them, of conquering a tricky piece of wood and persuading it into the shape she'd planned for it—so any deficiencies in communication between Matt and Kirra passed unnoticed.

She is nice, Kirra found herself thinking. I wonder if she has any idea of the true state of affairs between Matt and me? I wonder if he's told her he's going to marry me? She must be . . . curious, at least. Or perhaps she's used to him bringing different women down here . . .

It was after lunch that Min demonstrated she was

curious. Matt had disappeared towards the stables and Kirra was helping her with the clearing up when she said. 'You two . . . haven't known each other very long, have you? Oh, don't think I'm prying!' She rolled her eyes heavenwards, then grimaced and said honestly, 'Maybe I am. I . . . I've known Matt a long time, you see.'

'He . . .' Kirra hesitated, 'told me about you.'

Min's busy hands stilled on the sink briefly, then she started wiping it again. 'I'm glad,' she said quietly. 'Better to know now than find out later. If you're wondering what it means to us now, I can tell you that I shall always love Matt in a way, but not that way. That way,' she said with a sudden look of pain, 'is reserved for a man I can't have. That's why I'm here, trying to get myself together. Matt imagines I did him a favour once, and this is his way of repaying it. But if,' she paused, as if choosing her words with care, 'well, you find the situation bizzarre . . . I did try to explain to him when he rang me and told me he was bringing . . . someone down . . .' She stopped helplessly, then said very quietly, 'You're the first girl he's brought here, since I've been here, so I thought it must be . . . serious, and the last thing I wanted to do was . . . intrude.'

'You haven't,' Kirra heard herself say sincerely. 'This man—is there nothing—is he married to someone else?'

'He will be soon,' Min said carefully as she wiped and rewiped the already spotless sink. 'But not so long ago he was married to me.'

Kirra caught her breath and Min stopped wiping at last. And they looked at each other with the sudden and quite unspoken communion of two women in strife—as only women at the hands of men can be.

Kirra?' Min said uncertainly.

Kirra managed to smile shakily. 'I . . . I'm not very sure of myself sometimes, Min, that's all.'

'I'm sure Matt will help you to . . . overcome that. He . . . perhaps it's obvious I'm a bit of a fan,' Min said ruefully, 'but all the same . . .' She tapered off, then smiled suddenly. 'I'm sure he doesn't need me to speak for him! Would you like to see my work?'

'I'd love to see your work,' Kirra said, and went on to explain briefly what she did. 'I might be able to pass on some commissions or even find a buyer if you have any work for sale.'

Min tossed the dishcloth into the sink and said comically, 'Lady, you could be the answer to my prayers! Come, before you change your mind.'

Kirra bought three of Min's pieces on the spot, two statuettes and an intricately carved pair of bookends. They discussed what kind of work Min would be interested in doing if Kirra could pass it on.

'For example,' Kirra said, 'I know this sounds terribly commercial, but we're decorating a new house and the owner wants panels of frolicking dolphins set around the . . . er . . . jacuzzi—should I have even mentioned it?'

Min broke into peals of laughter and said finally, 'My dear Kirra, most artists are aware of the facts of life—dolphins about a jacuzzi are the bread-and-butter items that make it possible to go on and do your life's work. If you could send me some measurements, I'd be delighted to bone up on frolicking dolphins!'

Kirra left the studio after they had carefully packed

up the items she'd bought, and she left Min hunting through her books for pictures of dolphins.

There was no sign of Matt, and Kirra had a shower, changed into a primrose T-shirt and fresh jeans and packed her bag.

When there was still no sign of him, she wandered around downstairs for a while, then on an impulse climbed the staircase to his loft bedroom.

She hesitated at the top of the stairs, looking around. The big bed was made, the mulberry cover smooth, the desktop was neat and his bag stood open on a stool waiting to be packed. There was a stone fireplace at one end of the room surrounded by bookshelves, and she wandered over to it to inspect his literary tastes, which proved to be catholic, from Tolstoy to *The Hitch-Hiker's Guide to the Galaxy*—and there on one shelf all the books from his childhood.

She picked out *Jock of the Bushveld* and leafed through its yellowing pages and was enchanted by the drawings of animals on each page.

Then she wandered over to one of the dormer windows and sat down on the wooden window-seat with her feet up on it, knees bent, to savour the view.

How long she sat there she wasn't sure, but as she watched the afternoon darkened and heavy black clouds rolled down from Mount Warning, laying a shadow on everything and bringing an expectant still-ness to the afternoon.

It was as the first spots of rain spattered on to the stone of the terrace that she heard the outside door below open and close.

For some reason she didn't move, and she wondered if it was a sense of defiance that prompted her to stay

She turned her head from the view at last to see Matt at the top of the stairs, pausing, just realising she was there.

His eyebrows lifted, but all he said was, 'I thought you must be with Min.'

'I was,' she said and went to get up, but he came over to the window. The rain was now spearing down and hammering on the roof, the gutters were beginning to gurgle and forks of lightning were splitting the sky.

'Not scared?' he asked as a clap of thunder reverberated through the house.

She shook her head. 'I've always loved storms.'

'Stay there, then. I might as well pack. We'll leave as soon as the worst is over.'

He moved away and switched on a lamp, dispelling the shadows in the room and creating a warm circle of light against the uproar outside.

Kirra watched the storm for a bit longer, then she rested her head back and watched him instead. He was packing neatly and precisely, and he closed the bag and looked up, catching her gaze before she could look away. 'Did you come up here for any particular reason, Kirra?' he asked, his eyes suddenly intent and direct.

She stared at him then shook her head. 'Not really. As a matter of fact, I was trying to examine my motives as you came in.' Her lips twisted ruefully.

'Perhaps it was just plain curiosity?' he suggested.

'Perhaps,' she agreed.

'Of the type Bluebeard's den might arouse?' His look was slightly ironic.

'Hardly ' she said drily.

'Sometimes you look at me as if that's not at all hard to imagine.'

'Do I?' She shrugged.

He sat down in the armchair and sprawled his long legs out. 'Could I make a suggestion?'

'If it's a . . . make-love-not-war type of suggestion, no.'

He grinned and glanced at the smooth bed. 'There's a certain . . . added intimacy about making love in the middle of a crashing thunderstorm. Ever tried it?'

Kirra looked away, feeling sudden patches of heat on her throat and a dew of sweat along her hairline.

There was silence, until she said presently, 'I think the worst *is* over now.'

'Worst of what?' he asked, barely audibly, and she knew his eyes had not left her, nor had he missed the signs of her agitation.

'The storm is passing,' she said as equably as she was able, but thinking, I'll be damned if I'll acknowledge . . . anything!

'Let's go, then.'

'If you want to.' She looked at him at last, and was unable to mask the glint of defiance in her eyes.

CHAPTER SEVEN

'DAMN!' Kirra said suddenly, breaking the uneasy silence of the trip home. Matt had appeared as preoccupied as she was.

He turned his head and lifted an eyebrow. 'Forgotten something?'

'No. I mean, yes. It's Sunday . . . don't answer that.' She peered at her watch.

'It's five-thirty, it *is* Sunday—do you have a date?'

'Rupert and Mr Cassidy are coming over at six to . . .'

'Rupert? Mr Cassidy?' He shot her a laughing glance. 'Should I know about them as well?'

Kirra tightened her mouth, then said, 'Rupert is ten. He lives next door to me, with his parents and his dog—Mr Cassidy. We have a date to play Scrabble tonight. Any objections?'

'None. We should be there in plenty of time,' he said. 'I thought you said you hadn't had anything to do with children.'

'I said I hadn't had *much* to do with children—one child I baby-sit occasionally and play Scrabble with does not a summer make.'

'I stand corrected,' Matt replied gravely.

'Good,' Kirra said, but under her breath.

'What was that?'

'I'm glad you're capable of that, that's all,' she said sweetly.

'You must be feeling better,' he murmured. 'Either that, or there's something about my car that

120

brings out your fighting spirit.'

Kirra bit her lip and tried to force herself to relax. But she realised, as she turned her face to the window to watch the wet road reflect the lights as a premature, rain-laden dusk fell, that the weekend had taken a heavy toll of her, despite her resolution to indulge in no more histrionics or panicky manoeuvres. In fact, she felt as if her nerves were stretched to screaming-point, and it was almost impossible to squash the impulse to snap and be thoroughly bitchy.

'You don't have to come up,' she said stiffly when he pulled up outside her building.

'I don't intend to force myself on you,' he replied, and added with laughter lurking in his eyes, 'in this mood. All the same, you have rather a lot of stuff to carry, remember?'

She'd forgotten about Min's carvings. 'Oh . . . thanks,' she said briefly.

As they got out of the lift, two disconsolate figures further down the passage turned eagerly, one tail started to wag madly, then Kirra was besieged.

'You didn't forget!' Rupert cried enthusiastically.

'I'm afraid I did, Rupert—down, Mr Cassidy! I thought we had an arrangement about licking.'

'Then it's off.' Rupert's face fell, but almost immediately a spark of hope lit his eyes. 'Your friend could play with us! Three makes it even better, and I've added two new words to my list . . . one game, just one,' he entreated.

Mr Cassidy, who was small, black and white in some parts and brindle in others, and whose pedigree was hard to imagine, barked excitedly.

Matt said, 'I'm a fair Scrabble player myself.'

Kirra flashed him a look, then said resignedly, 'All right, inside you lot!'

* * *

'I know who you are,' Rupert remarked to Matt some time later.

'Oh?'

'You're the man with the smashing Rolls. I saw you pick Kirra up yesterday. Are you—oh, bother!' he said, noticing that Kirra had won the game. 'I didn't get the chance to use either of my new words!'

'Next time,' Kirra said consolingly. 'It was my turn to get all the good letters today.'

'She's pretty good at this game,' Rupert confided ruefully to Matt. 'Is she going to marry you instead of Jeremy?'

Kirra flushed and avoided Matt's wry look. 'Rupert,' she began but Matt said, 'Perhaps.'

Rupert grimaced. 'I was hoping no one would until I was old enough to marry her myself, but I don't suppose I can be expected to compete with a bloke with a Rolls-Royce, can I?'

Kirra closed her mouth, floored again in the space of a moment, but Rupert had suddenly turned bright red and was looking as if he heartily wished the ground would open up beneath his feet, so she put aside all other sentiments to say gravely as she ruffled his hair, 'Thank you for that, Rupe.'

'You don't . . .' He got stuck.

'I think, in fact I know,' she said with a slight smile, 'that all girls, even when it's not possible, appreciate a compliment like that, really they do.'

Rupert looked relieved then the phone rang once, his parents' signal that it was time to go home, and he and Mr Cassidy left, not without some good-natured grumbling.

Kirra closed the door on them and leant back against it, feeling exhausted. There was still Matt to be dealt with—he'd sent her the most wicked glance during Rupert's unexpected revelations, and she hadn't dared to look at him since.

He was standing with his back to her, staring out of the window, so she picked up the tray of refreshments she had provided and took it into the kitchen. But her nerves were beginning to get the better of her again, she discovered, as she put the biscuit-barrel away with unwanted force, rammed the glasses into the dishwasher and wiped the clean kitchen sink until she reminded herself of Min. She threw the cloth away disgustedly and, muttering beneath her breath, turned to march back into the lounge, only to bump into the subject of her ire—who was lounging in the doorway.

'Steady on,' he said softly, straightening and catching her about the waist.

'Let me go.' Her eyes were stormy.

'In a moment. So you have . . . another admirer?'

'Possibly a more genuine one!' she flashed at him.

He looked amused and drew her a fraction closer. 'Time will tell.'

'I'm sure you're right,' she said tautly. 'May I make a request?'

He thought for a moment, then said, 'Sure. I'm . . . definitely open to requests.' His words were husky and almost caressing, as were his hands, moving up from her waist to span her back beneath her shoulders. She tried to break away, but he pulled her closer and leant back against the door-frame, eyeing her mutinously set mouth with a perfectly grave expression that was a mockery in itself. 'Fire away.'

'I would . . .' she said raggedly, 'I would like you to go away and leave me alone for a while.'

'Is the strain getting to you, Kirra?' he asked.

'I . . .'

'Or would you like a little time to . . . reconnoitre?' He lowered his eyelids as he inspected the hollows at the base of her throat just above the neckline of the primrose T-shirt.

'Yes,' she said before she could stop herself.

His lashes lifted leisurely and her heart started to beat faster, but he smiled faintly and said placidly, 'I'll be interested to see what you come up with between now and Friday. I'll be in Melbourne until Thursday, by the way, but I thought we might go out on Friday night.' He lifted an eyebrow at her.

'If . . . if you want to,' she said helplessly.

'Oh, I do. Incidentally, what kind of a ring would you like for your third engagement ring? Do you like sapphires?'

'I hate sapphires,' Kirra said precisely. 'My first engagement ring was a sapphire, as it happens.'

'Dear me,' he replied, 'it hadn't occurred to me but that's obviously a problem for such a much engaged lady as yourself. Let's see . . . if we rule out diamonds and sapphires, what's left? A ruby? Or an emerald?'

'I've a much better idea,' Kirra said through her teeth. 'Why don't you get me a ring replica of a ball and chain?'

He laughed softly and bent his head to kiss her lightly on the lips. *'Touché!* See you Friday.' He released her and left without another word.

'Darling, I'll be fine,' Kirra said into the phone on Wednesday evening. 'I think it's a great idea for you and Dad to have a break, and if he's agreeable, you should definitely strike while the iron's hot so to speak. He could change his mind.'

'Well, I know it's a bit of an out-of-the-blue

decision,' Naomi said down the line, 'but I do think he needs to get away, and we thought we'd just get into the car tomorrow morning and head for wherever the mood takes us.'

'Sounds lovely,' Kirra said warmly. 'Just don't spoil it worrying about me or anything. There isn't——' She paused. 'There's nothing to worry about any more, is there?' She tried to sound casual.

'Not a thing,' Naomi replied, 'but sometimes it's very hard to wind down, if you know what I mean.'

'Mmm . . . Of course, it's not all completely finalised yet, is it?' said Kirra. 'I mean, it must take time to draw up all the contracts and so on.' For some reason she held her breath as she waited.

Naomi chuckled. 'Actually, it's all signed and sealed, pet, and what's more, Matt has already sunk a substantial amount of capital into Munro's. Apparently it's a well-known fact in the business world that once he decides to move, he moves very swiftly, but I must say your father was quite surprised at the speed of things. But then . . .'

'Mum,' Kirra stared at herself in the mirror above the phone table and saw she was white with shock, 'when . . . you didn't mention this . . .'

'About the contracts? Didn't we?' Naomi said vaguely, then, on a sharper note, 'You haven't been worrying still, have you, Kirralee? The contracts were a formality once we had his word. He . . . he's that kind of a man, my dear, and . . . well, I suppose we just never guessed you might be afraid . . .'

Kirra didn't hear the rest of what her mother was saying nor, as she put the phone down, did she remember what she had said in reply, but it must have reassured her mother because her parting words had been cheerful, that she did know. But as she stared at her still pale, shocked and disbelieving face in the mirror, a tide of understanding began to course through her, and a tide of rage . . .

CHAPTER EIGHT

'OH . . .'

She moved away from the phone at last, breathing heavily, and discovered that her hands were shaking and her thoughts were flying in a dozen different directions, only to be pulled back like a ball on a string . . .

'All along it *was* a game, a cold, cruelly calculated game of revenge, but he must have known I could have found out . . . he can't have cared! Perhaps he counted each succeeding day I remained in ignorance as a bonus after the initial fright he gave me, and he had a few weeks up his sleeve, anyway . . . oh! And he was probably clever enough to realise my old-fashioned parents would place more trust in his word than pieces of paper . . . I could have gone on in ignorance for *weeks* longer! But *why*?'

She stood in the middle of her lounge, examining all the answers she could command. 'He's a devil, a cold, cynical . . . devil beneath the charm and the . . . He had to be, because what I did to him was nothing compared to this. What did I do, anyway? Get a bit carried away for a few hours, but *this* . . .'

She started to pace the room agitatedly, trying to bring some order to the angry chaos of her thoughts, some logic to his actions. 'To think,' she whispered, 'That I even began to wonder if I'd fallen in love with him . . . Oh, I see, damn you, Matthew Remington!' she breathed. 'That's what you were planning to achieve, not for the pleasure of having me chained in a one-sided marriage to you, but for the pleasure of being able to walk away from me. How subtle and tortuous, but don't imagine . . .'

The phone rang, and for a moment she was tempted to ignore it, then she strode across the room and lifted it impatiently. It was a long-distance call, and an operator asked for Miss Kirra Munro, then connected her to Mr Remington.

Kirra's eyes flashed with fire through a series of clicks, then narrowed almost calculatingly.

'Kirra?' His voice came down the line.

'H-hello?' she said unsteadily, because she was thinking furiously.

'Were you asleep?'

'No! I mean, no . . .'

'You sound bemused.'

'I didn't think you knew my number,' she said lamely.

'I didn't, but it was simple enough to find it. Do you mind me ringing you?'

'I . . . are you still in Melbourne?'

'Yes—and thinking of you.'

Kirra was silent, amazed that, despite all she now knew, her skin was prickling, not only at what he had said, but because she thought he sounded tired.

'Kirra?'

'I'm here.' She cleared her throat. 'Have you been very busy?'

'Yes. Have you?'

'No . . . uh . . . just normal.'

'Have you come to any more conclusions about us?' he queried.

Kirra clenched her free fist, but managed to say, 'There doesn't seem to be any point, does there, beyond . . . upsetting myself.'

'I'm glad to hear you say so. I thought you might have decided to leave the country after our last encounter.'

'What would you do if I did . . . do that?'

'I think you know that,' he said after a pause.

'Of course.' Her eyes gleamed. 'Just . . . checking the state of the art.'

'If we were together, the state of the art would be . . .'

'Don't,' she broke in wearily.

'Would be infinitely pleasing, as we both know, and despite your intention to fight it,' he said deliberately. Then he added flatly, 'I'm missing you for what it's worth.'

Liar, she found herself wanting to say, to shout. She said instead, 'What's that supposed to mean?'

He took his time about answering. 'That I'd like to be with you, holding you, touching and exploring . . . making love to you. That's all.'

'All?' Her voice quivered, and not only with scepticism, but because his words had undoubtedly exposed a nerve, damn him again, she thought.

'Is there more?' he asked. 'Something I missed?'

'You . . . ' She took a breath. 'Why don't you go to bed? You sound tired.'

'So do you—tired and scratchy. We could be missing each other. Personally, I think I'm going to stay up and work. If six o'clock suits you, I'll see you then. Sweet dreams, Kirra.' The phone clicked in her ear.

She put it down slowly and carefully, lost in thought. Then she shook herself mentally and went to bed, but there were no sweet dreams for her, there were too many plans to be made, too much to review. For example, having made the decision that two could play games, and that it might even be possible for a late starter to turn the tables, there was also to be decided how she should carry on so that he wouldn't suspect she knew, until it was too late.

On the whole it would be wisest not to change too much, she told herself. If you suddenly become all sultry and seductive, he's going to smell a rat. No, Kirra, it's your turn to be . . . subtle.

It wasn't until the early hours of the morning, when she was light-headed with tiredness, that the irony of the situation occurred to her. Instead of being immeasurably relieved, she was immeasurably hostile and hell-bent on revenge.

'But why shouldn't I?' she asked herself, turning her cheek to the pillow wearily. 'Why should I weakly and spinelessly accept being made such a fool of?'

At six o'clock precisely on Friday evening, her doorbell rang, and it was more by accident than design that her plan of action received the boost it needed. She had actually planned to step out of the shower to answer the door; what she hadn't anticipated was that she would have had an exceedingly busy two days, that she would be genuinely delayed at work by a talkative client, genuinely feel the need to dive into the shower because it had been a hot, muggy afternoon, and genuinely feel rushed and tense and tired as she opened the door with dripping hair and a damp robe clutched awkwardly round her equally damp body.

In spite of that, he managed to surprise her.

'Hello . . . oh!' she said, blinking as she took in the fact that he was wearing shorts and sand shoes, and that he appeared to be laden down with packages,

Not only that—he looked casual and carefree, younger, bigger . . . but not in the least like the satanic monster her overwrought imagination had turned him into.

He raised an eyebrow lazily. 'You look surprised to see me, Kirra.'

'I'm not . . . I'm . . . I just got home and it's been so hot. Um . . . come in,' she said confusedly, turning away and leaving him to close the door with his heel.

There was evidence of her late arrival home in the form of her bag, open and spilling its contents, and two carrier-bags tossed down on the settee, a pair of earrings and her sun-glasses on the glass-topped table, her elegant navy shoes discarded on the carpet, her mail, still unopened lying on the floor beside them where she had dropped it in her haste. She knelt down to gather it up, muttering beneath her breath.

When she stood up, he had deposited his packages on the dining-room table and was standing right behind her, causing her to mutter something else as she turned and bumped into him.

His lips twisted as he took her by the shoulders to steady her, and he murmured, 'Busy day, by the look of it,' as she juggled the mail and the sash of her robe which had slipped loose.

She nodded perfunctorily. 'I'll just go and . . . get decent.'

'Decent?' he said softly, his hazel eyes following the little trails of water sliding down her neck and trickling into the valley between her breasts which were now outlined quite clearly beneath the damp, clinging silk.

Kirra swallowed and knew she could do one of two things—break away now, or pretend to be mesmerised and let him have his way . . . up to a point.

She trembled and stared up at him, hoping no flicker of her indecision showed in her eyes, yet wondering what he would expect to see—how she could project a genuinely helpless submission to this moment that had somehow exceeded her plans and expectations.

'I . . .' It was only a breath of sound and her lips closed then quivered as he slid one hand down her robe and laid his forefinger unerringly on the slight mound of her nipple beneath the silk.

If he had branded her, she thought later, the effect could hardly have been more electrifying. All her senses leapt and both her nipples hardened into taut peaks, her eyes widened in surprise, and she dropped the mail again.

'Like that?' he asked, his hazel gaze capturing hers as he circled the throbbing bud of her nipple with his finger and slid his arm around her shoulders.

Kirra closed her eyes and unwittingly laid her head back against his arm. 'Yes,' she gasped as his fingers moved to her other breast, caressingly, circling first then touching the peak so that she shuddered.

'And this?' He bent his head and kissed her throat, sliding his lips down the smooth skin to the hollows at the base of her neck, tasting her at the same time as he slid his hand through her hair, exploring the tender skin of her nape and behind her ears. And his other hand left her breasts and slid around her hips, drawing her into him, moulding her body to the strength and hardness of his.

Kirra whispered something inaudible, perhaps despairing, as she felt herself softening against him, and she tried to concentrate on the fact that she must retain some control, however subtle, of the situation.

But her mind seemed to be moving very slowly, as slowly as his hands were moving on her body, and it was almost impossible to concentrate on anything but the lovely sensations that were running through her, the feel of *him*, the need to respond . . .

She raised her arms and spread her hands on his back, feeling the long muscles through his thin shirt, and she opened her eyes as he lifted his head, and knew he was going to claim her mouth, and that she would not resist.

It was a kiss that left her shuddering in his arms, every nerve-ending quivering, a kiss that left her mouth feeling bruised but her body aching for this intimacy to continue, as if it were a primitive force flowing between them that could not be denied. What surprised her dimly, as she stared up into his eyes, was the absence of any look of triumph.

'Kirra?' His lips barely moved.

'What?' she whispered, but she knew the exact nature of the enquiry in his eyes—or perhaps it was a statement, she thought then, of his undoubted desire for her. He was breathing heavily, she could see, and there was a nerve beating in his jaw, and he was holding her against him still, as if the feel of her body on his was irresistible.

I've got him right where I want him, the thought skimmed her mind, but it was followed immediately by a more honest one—we're in the same boat, and what I'm going to do now is, curiously, what I would have done before I found out, and for the same reason . . .

She lowered her head and rested her brow on his shoulder for a brief moment. Then her body slackened and she dropped her hands to her sides. And she returned his gaze with her blue-grey eyes sombre but steady.

His mouth tightened into a hard line for a second, then he released her abruptly and stepped back and said, 'Is this where I take refuge in a cold shower?'

Kirra licked her lips and stared down at the sash of her robe which she'd started to pleat unconsciously. 'We could go for a swim,' she said with an effort.

He smiled without humour. 'In the dark?'

'It won't be dark for another half-hour.'

'I should have had the foresight to bring some togs,' he said ironically.

'What . . . what did you bring?'

'Dinner,' he said laconically, glancing at the packages on her dining-room table. 'Take-away Italian we could heat up. All right, if you don't mind me going around in damp shorts, let's go.'

'I . . .'

'This was your idea, Kirra.'

She saw the merciless glint in his hazel eyes and turned away defensively.

It was beautiful on the beach, and by mutual, unspoken consent they walked for a while first, before taking the plunge. The water was cold at first, then the buffeting of the surf was refreshing yet relaxing at the same time. At least, when they came out, at the western horizon was a pure fiery orange streaked with feathery dark clouds, Kirra wrapped her towel around her and found herself feeling tense, although they still had not exchanged a word.

She stared around as Matt dried himself then slung the towel round his neck, and she wondered if the swim had achieved anything for him. And she explored the errant thought that she couldn't help wishing things were simple between them, as clean cut and beautiful as this beach in the sunset, the sea, the sky . . . two people with this undoubted craving for each other's bodies. Surely, she thought, there must be an answering hunger in our souls. But . . .

Her lips parted as a sudden flash of fear gripped her heart, the forerunner of a curious premonition which caused her to plead with herself . . . no, oh, no, not that. *Remember* all he's put you through . . .

'Kirra?'

She blinked and looked up at him, and he took her chin in his hand, his hazel eyes acute and very probing, and the irrational fear that he might be able to see into the depths of her soul, might even be able to mould all her fears and uncertainties into the consequence she knew she could only dread and regret, gave her back her spirit of defiance and hostility, although she was quick to veil it from her eyes.

'I don't know about you, but I'm hungry,' she said huskily. 'I missed out on lunch.'

His eyes narrowed and his fingers on her chin tightened briefly; she shivered slightly but inwardly, because she knew the gauntlet she had thrown down had been picked up, and that the rest of the evening would be a battle of wits from which she could emerge mentally scarred and bleeding if she wasn't cool and cautious—and committed to her cause. She knew, and it gave her a moment's pause, that one of the reasons they could fight this battle at all was that they were beginning to know each other rather well, perhaps too well . . .

She wasn't sure why this should disturb her, like some dark wings brushing her mind, and anyway the thought was so elusive, she had to let it go. And she waited, with patience, for his reaction.

He released her chin. 'Let's eat, then, Miss

Munro,' he said.

'I think I'll have another shower, a quick one,' she said casually when they got back. 'To wash the salt out of my hair. Would you like one?'

He looked at her speculatively. 'No. Just a dry towel, thanks.'

'Oh!' She glanced at his damp shorts. 'If you give those to me, I'll put them in the dryer—they won't take long.'

'Thank you,' he said with a slightly ironic look. 'If you're sure your . . . principles won't feel compromised if I wander around for a while in only a towel?'

'No, they won't,' she replied with deliberate lightness. 'Nor will any of my chairs bear damp patches. Do you think your poor, wounded masculine pride will ever recover?'

She couldn't help the secret little smile of amusement that curved her lips at the cutting hazel glance that flashed her way, but if she thought she'd scored a direct hit, he made an almost instantaneous recovery. He grimaced and said wryly, 'I know now how Mr Cassidy must feel.'

Kirra raised her eyebrows.

'Yes,' he said softly. 'What was it you said to him? "Down, dog—I thought we had an agreement about licking." Or words to that effect. Is that the same technique you used on Jeremy?'

'Jeremy . . .' Kirra bit her lip. 'Let's leave him out of this,' she said quietly.

He shrugged. 'If you prefer. Why don't you go and have that shower? I'll start heating up our dinner.'

Kirra hesitated.

'I'm quite domesticated,' he murmured.

She turned on her heel and left him.

She put on a pair of white shorts and a blue and white sleeveless sailor blouse after her shower, and left her hair loose to dry. While she was tidying up the bedroom, she heard the dryer going on and was annoyed for a second at the thought of him making himself at home in her laundry as well as her kitchen, but she resolutely banished any suggestion of pettiness, and paused to wonder what she had achieved so far tonight. And, with a feathery feeling of apprehension, it occurred to her that rejecting Matt was like playing with fire. But at least I've stated my case, and the fact that he's not forcing me to marry him is immaterial. Once more, though, how to go on? Perhaps I can only play it by ear . . .

When she emerged from the bedroom, it was to see the low glass-topped table in the lounge set with cutlery and two napkins, wineglasses, a dish of parmesan cheese and a salad. She raised an eyebrow and went into the kitchen.

He'd bought canelloni and he was dishing it out of the foil containers as she came in. She couldn't help sniffing appreciatively.

'Smells good, doesn't it?'

'Smells delicious,'she agreed.

'Do you mind if we eat in the lounge?'

'Not at all. We can watch the news or whatever's on. I'll bring the wine.' He had even, she noticed, filled her silver bucket with ice, and the wine was in it, already opened.

They ate sitting side by side on the settee, and thanks to *The Good Life*, which happened to be on television, Kirra was able to relax and even laugh a little.

'That was an old one but a good one,' she said,

pushing away her plate and leaning back with her wineglass.

Matt stood up and collected the plates.

'I'll do the dishes later,' she said, but he took no notice, leaving only the wine behind, and she heard the tap running in the kitchen as he rinsed everything.

She stood up herself after a couple of minutes, to change the television channel, but nothing appealed and she switched it off and listened to the relative silence. This was broken by the sound of the dryer door opening, and she wondered if he was leaving.

He certainly re-appeared wearing his shorts instead of a towel, but as their gazes caught and held across the room her skin prickled and she felt the tension building up again, and she knew the second—or was it the third—round of this bout was set to begin.

She bent her head briefly, then looked up at him and said quietly, 'What now?'

He strolled over to the settee, poured more wine into both their glasses and sat down with his. 'You choose—I'm easy.' He raised his glass in a mocking little toast.

Kirra tried to compose her thoughts, and finally could only fall back on honesty. She pushed her hair back wearily. 'It would be nice just to relax.'

He raised an eyebrow. 'Do you think it's possible?'

'I . . . it *should* be,' she said with a sudden intensity that took even her by surprise.

'Care to sit down and elaborate?' he queried.

'If you intend to,' she started to say tautly, 'to . . .'

'I don't intend to *force* my attentions on you, Kirra,' he drawled.

She bit her lip frustratedly, then sat down with a fair length of the settee between them, and picked up her glass. 'Perhaps what I'm trying to say is this,' she stared down at the glass in her hand then raised her eyes to his, 'if a marriage is not to be the kind of shambles your parents had, there have to be times when you can relax together in tenderness and affection and . . . tolerance and humour.'

'Sure,' he agreed. 'After the loving—and it's possible to have those things between a man and a woman outside of marriage . . .'

'We're not talking about that,' Kirra broke in.

'If I am, it's to make you aware I am capable of that,' he said deliberately.

'But only *after* the loving,' Kirra said ironically. 'Or to be more specific, the sex.'

He shrugged. 'It's generally what generates those other feelings.'

'If,' Kirra said slowly, 'we went to bed now, say, and we found it didn't generate the rest, would you release me from our . . . contract?'

'No.' His gaze was slightly amused, mostly enigamtic.

'Just . . . no?'

'I'm afraid so.'

'And you're not at all afraid it will be that kind of a shambles?' she asked meditatively.

He thought for a moment, then said, 'The elements of my parents' marriage that made it such a mess will be lacking in ours, Kirra, because we're making a commitment to marriage.'

She laid her head back. 'Not to each other, but to the institution, in other words. Wouldn't it be strange if we fell in love one day?'

He was silent for so long, she turned her head to look at him at last, to surprise an oddly grim look in his eyes. 'Of course, you don't believe in that, do you?' she said softly. 'It's sentimental fairy-tale to you, whereas to me . . .' She paused. 'Do you know what the main difference between us is?' she asked then, and went on without waiting for a reply, 'You mistrust the emotional side of love, while I mistrust the physical side. If ever the twain were to meet . . . who knows what the outcome would be.'

'What are you trying to say, Kirra?' he said at last with a faint frown.

'I'm just . . . meditating, I guess. Just as I can't help meditating about sleeping with you, sometimes, to be perfectly honest. And how my famous inhibitions would react. Whether you could turn my rather timid inexperience into the kind of naked desire that would match yours.'

'There's one way to find that out,' he said, barely audibly.

'Yes,' she agreed, but almost absently. 'Do you ever wonder what it will be like to have the responsibility for the well-being, the real well-being of a woman on your hands? Have you ever thought of it like that?'

'Have you?'

'Yes, I have—lately I've thought of it quite a lot. Perhaps they're not very emancipated or liberated thoughts to have, but then in my case, I'm not in a very liberated situation. You're expecting me to . . . put my life in your hands, to regard you as my anchor, my solace through the years and pain of childbearing and rearing and growing old. If I were to tell you that the thought of going through all that without the prospect of you finding any joy, real joy in me, is . . .' She broke off and shivered, and sat up abruptly.

'Kirra,' he said harshly, 'you were all set to do that

to yourself only months ago.'

'Yes,' she whispered and turned to stare at him gravely. 'You've certainly . . . taught me a few lessons about myself one way or another, Matt,' she said huskily, and added, 'the hard way. Would you like a cup of coffee?'

'No.' He reached over and took her wrist. 'Don't run away now.'

'I'm not. Where is there to run?'

'Tell me this, then—if I weren't forcing you to marry me, would you sleep with me now, Kirra?' His eyes held hers and they were grim again, and his fingers hard on her wrists.

'Is that all you ever think of?'

'And you don't? You just told me you did.'

'I . . .' She took an uncertain breath.

'Would you?' he persisted.

'No.'

'Just . . . no?' he mimicked.

'I'd be mad to, wouldn't I, Matt?' she said very steadily, suddenly finding her thoughts crystallising to a degree of stunning clarity. 'What then would be the difference between me and all those women who latched on to your father, all the women, for all I know, who've done the same to you? What prospects would I have of not being loved and—left?

'You know, all the lessons haven't only been self-revealing. They've taught me something else—you've despised a lot of women for doing just that—sleeping with you in seemingly casual circumstances, but perhaps hoping to pin you down. Oh no, and with all I know, of you were asking me to marry you, I'd be mad to do that as well.'

'Those are very lofty sentiments, Kirra.'

'What's the point of going through the mill if you

don't aim for something higher?' she retorted and added, 'I gather you're not going to defend the charges.'

He smiled for the first time, a cool, slow smile. 'No. What you said is probably true to a degree. Incidentally, you're putting up a great fight, my dear.' He released her wrist, and added softly, 'Even better than I expected. There is just this to consider. You're going to have to sleep with me sooner or later —don't make things too hard for yourself when the time comes, will you?'

Kirra stared at him and said equally softly, and with a curious glint in her blue-grey eyes, 'I'll make things as hard as I can—for both of us.'

His lips twisted. 'That's my Kirra,' he said and stood up. 'I'm off to Adelaide for a few days, incidentally. I'll be in touch as soon as I get back. Any . . . last thoughts you'd care to add?'

'No. Have you?'

He narrowed his eyes and searched her still, slightly pale face probingly. And when he said he hadn't, Kirra got the impression he'd been about to say something else and changed his mind, and for some reason her skin prickled again and those same elusive thoughts she had encountered on the beach brushed her mind but remained as elusive.

He left without attempting to touch her, although something, she thought, had flowed between them. Some indefinable current that she could only dimly identify as the binding of two enemies locked on a collision course and, even in their discord, or perhaps because of it, acutely aware of each other.

She took the thought to bed with her, turning it over and over in her mind and asking herself why she should be preoccupied with it instead of, for instance, how well she was succeeding in turning the tables on him.

The days passed until nearly a week had gone by with no word from him and as they passed she became restless and edgy, and even began to wonder if he was playing hard to get. That it should occupy her thoughts to the degree it was concerned her, but, when his secretary rang her and spoke to her with distant hauteur, another possibility occurred to Kirra —and had the effect of temporarily enraging her.

CHAPTER NINE

'MISS MUNRO? Miss Kirra Munro?'

'Yes?' Kirra said into the phone, just before she was due to leave for work.

'It's June Daly here, Mr Remington's private secretary. He's asked me to advise you that he's been delayed in Adelaide—not to mention indisposed.' The last part was said reprovingly.

'Indisposed?'

'Er . . . yes, a virus by the sound of it. What he needs is a holiday, but he doesn't take the slightest notice of me. Be that as it may, he said he would call you when it was possible.'

Don't call us, we'll call you . . . The phrase shot through Kirra's mind. I wonder . . .

'Is . . . is he on the coast?' she asked, managing to sound almost diffident as her brian worked overtime.

'He gets in at lunch time.'

'Well, thank you . . . oh! I wonder if I could have this address.' How ridiculous, she thought. I don't even know where he lives.

'I'm afraid it's not my place to hand out Mr Remington's address,' said June Daly stiffly.

'I was only . . . thinking of sending him some fruit to . . . cheer him up,' Kirra said, improvising madly.'

'If you'd like to send it to the office, Miss Munro, I'll see it gets passed on.'

'How kind of you!' Kirra said brightly. 'Thank

you,' But it was with a great effort that she restrained herself from slamming down the phone. Yet it was more than June Daly's manner —although Kirra did think briefly, How dare she? Who the hell does she think she is? that caused Kirra's eyes to glint with anger and her fists to clench so that her nails dug into her palms. It was the thought that Matt Remington might be choosing to end the farce before she'd had the pleasure of getting her own back.

'Well, well,' she whispered, 'we'll have to see about that.' And she picked up the phone again and rang Stanley.

'Stanley—do you think Dad would have made a note of Mr Remington's home address? I—er —I've been invited to a party and I'd like to ask him.' This was true enough—it was Marcus and Pippa's house-warming on Sunday night, and they would undoubtedly be delighted if she took Matthew Remington—they just didn't know it yet.

'I can tell you that, Kirra,' Stanley said down the line. 'Your father got me to deliver some papers to him one night. Uh . . . it's the Biarritz building, Old Burleigh Road, and it's number . . .'

Kirra wrote the number down carefully. 'Fancy that,' she murmured. 'I know it well.' Then she thanked Stanley and mentioned she'd had a card from her parents and that they seemed to be enjoying themselves.

She thought for a bit after putting down the phone, then went off to work.

The Biarritz apartment building was situated slightly removed from the high-rise jungle of Surfers' and the streets around it were quiet and leafy. As the sun set, Kirra entered the luxurious lobby and took the lift to the fourteenth floor with a distinct feeling of *déjà vu*. The feeling was heightened as she stepped out of the lift and looked around, because she was almost sure the number she sought would be on a door that would open up to marble floors faintly pink-tinged in the lounge and dining-room, a wall of mirrors, marble tables, beautiful rugs, a plain white couch and two Chinese chairs with brass inlays and yellow velvet seats, duplicated in the dining-room suite, a pristine white kitchen.

She knocked on the door and waited, wondering what she would do if he wasn't home.

He was.

It was hard to say who was more taken aback as he opened the door. Kirra was certainly surprised at the way he looked, his eyes heavy-lidded, his face lined in a way that made him look older, blue shadows on his jaw. He'd discarded the jacket of a dark blue suit, and his shirt sleeves were half rolled up untidily, and his tie loosened.

He also, after a blink of surprise to see her on his doorstep, looked distinctly unenthusiastic, which caused her to tighten her lips momentarily as he said, 'Kirra—what are you doing here?'

'I heard you were . . . indisposed.'

'Who the hell told you that?'

'Your Miss Daly—or perhaps it's Mrs Daly. She sounded cross because you always disregard her advice, about taking holidays, for example.'

He looked irritated beyond words. 'She tries to mother me, and I didn't ask her to tell you I was sick which I'm not.'

'You don't look very well.'

'That's none of her business, and besides . . . '

'Oh, don't worry. She wouldn't reveal your address. I had to scrounge around for that! But seriously, you don't . . .'

'Now, don't *you* start, Kirra.'

'Do we have to conduct this conversation on the doorstep?' she broke in. 'We are engaged to be married, after all,' she added sweetly.

He stared at her, then moved aside to let her in.

Nothing had been changed in the main rooms, she saw, which struck her as ironic. And an open leather briefcase stood on the floor beside the dining-room table which was littered with papers.

'You're not still working?' Kirra asked, observing this together with the silver pen and his gold-rimmed glasses, which looked as if they had been flung down impatiently.

'Why not?' he countered. 'If you've come to play Florence Nightingale, I told you I'm not . . .'

'Were you sick?' she asked coolly.

He shrugged. 'It was only one of those twenty-four hour viruses.'

'Which leaves you feeling like death warmed up, and looking it,' she supplied. 'Have you eaten this evening?'

'Not . . . yet.'

'Then I'll make you something,' she said quietly. 'And don't argue with me, please. If it's all right for you to take out my splinters—and feed me—it's all right for me to do this. Call it reciprocity, if you like.'

He grimaced, then grinned twistedly. 'I don't know that I've got anything much to make.'

She lifted up her string bag and put it on the kitchen counter. 'I came prepared,' she said calmly. 'Provided it doesn't take too long, you could finish off what you're doing—then clear it up.'

He hesitated briefly, then said ruefully, 'Yes, sir.'

Kirra had bought seasoned chicken breasts which she fried until they were crisp and golden, and a carton of cooked rice and raisins and nuts that she warmed up. She made a fresh salad, then looked around for a cheese-board but had to make do with a large platter for the smoked cheese she had bought with biscuits, two juicy nectarines and a bunch of grapes. The state of his cupboards and fridge spoke volumes—he rarely ate at home. Her other purchase had been a crusty loaf of bread.

She went unerringly to the linen cupboard for a tablecloth and napkins and just before she dished up, to the guest bathroom.

'You seem to know your way around here, Kirra,' he said thoughtfully, as she set the meal out on the table.

'I do. I helped decorate it.'

'So,' he said, unfurling his napkin and shooting her a hazel, lazy glance, 'I've virtually been living with a part of you ever since I bought the place—it was newly decorated when I bought it. That's rather ironic, isn't it?'

She could only agree, but said, 'I didn't do it all. But I did find the Chinese chairs and the lamps and —if it's still in the main bedroom, the painting.' She stopped abruptly, because that particular painting was of a half-naked woman with only a gauzy skirt on, rising up out of a flowery meadowland. It had been a half-humorous touch on Kirra's part, but she'd also thought it was beautifully done, hazy but with a lovely quality of light and pearly skin tones.

For the first time that evening, as she looked across at him with a tinge of defiance, she read genuine amusement in his eyes, and he said softly, 'She's still there to tantalise me from time to time.'

Kirra coloured and, to cover it, implemented the next part of her plan. 'Do you think you'll be one hundred per cent by Sunday?'

'Of course. Why?' He looked at her enquiringly.

'I've been invited to a party.'

He pushed his plate away. 'That was very nice. Thanks.'

'Well?' she asked with a challenging gleam in her eye that she couldn't quite hide.

He leant back in his chair, one hand on the table fiddling absently with a spoon. 'What kind of a party?'

'Very elegant, I've no doubt.' She caught herself sounding sardonic and went on swiftly, 'It's a house-warming, they're rather good friends of mine. He's an architect and she's an old school-friend.'

'Have you told them about us?'

'No.'

'Do you intend to?'

'Not on Sunday night. Is there some reason why you'd rather not come? They know a lot of the best people.'

For an instant she thought she saw a flicker of contempt in his eyes, then it was gone. Still, it was with a rather dry smile that he said, 'It appears to me you've changed tactics, Kirra. If I seem reluctant, it's because I can't help wondering what you're up to.'

'Tactics?' she said softly, but with a little flame of anger causing her eyes to look bluer. 'I can't imagine why I didn't think of indulging in them sooner! Still, I'm learning. It must be,' she smiled, 'from . . . associating with a master tactician like yourself.'

He said nothing, but studied her dispassionately for a time. Then he remarked almost grimly, 'If you're regretting the physical closeness we achieved last time we met, in spite of our differences . . .'

'Oh, I am,' she broke in. 'You've hit the nail on the head.'

He didn't respond, just kept turning the spoon over and over in his long fingers. Then he dropped it and rubbed his forehead briefly.

Kirra stared at him, then said reluctantly, 'Have you . . . got a headache?'

He shrugged.

'Have you *taken* anything for it?'

'I will . . . all right, I'll come to the . . . party.' Something glinted in his eyes she couldn't decipher. 'What time would you care to be collected, Miss Munro?'

Kirra bit her lip, then shot him a dark look. 'Seven, but only if you feel up to it.' She got up and gathered some plates. 'Would there be anything like a simple aspirin around?'

He looked amused and pointed to a kitchen cupboard. She got out two and took them to him with a glass of water. 'Don't . . . just don't argue,' she warned him wearily. 'Is there anything else you'd like? A cup of tea?'

He nodded after a moment.

She was just pouring it when she heard his chair scrape back, and tensed as he came into the kitchen. But he didn't touch her, just leant back against the counter and folded his arms.

Then he said, with a smile twisting his lips, 'So you came here to fight with me tonight, not smother me with tender loving care, Kirra.'

'I did cook you a meal,' she pointed out. 'Here's your tea. Why don't you take it into the lounge while I clear up?'

'I would certainly hesitate to do anything else with you in this mood of extreme militancy,' he said. 'Except to assure you that by Sunday I should be . . . fighting fit.'

Kirra looked at him expressionlessly.

'Unless,' he said softly, 'you'd like to come to bed with me now? That might restore me better than anything else.'

'Take your tea and go,' she advised him.

'Small comfort,' he said with a wry twitch of his lips, but he did as he was told.

She watched him as he strolled into the lounge, put his cup down and pulled off his tie. Then she switched her gaze back to the task at hand.

Ten minutes later, she glanced over the counter again to see that he'd fallen asleep sprawled back on the settee. She finished off as quietly as she could and moved around switching off all the lamp but one, then stood staring down at him.

Sleep, she saw, had smoothed away the lines of weariness and strain, and it occurred to her that her rush of emotion as to whether she was being 'brushed off' might have been misplaced. Well, in this instance, at least, she mused. He's obviously been ill and he's just as obviously very tired. He also might be one of those men who genuinely hate being fussed over when they're sick.

Then she discovered how hard it was to tear her
gaze away and her heart started to beat heavily, so
heavily that she sat down in the Chinese chair
beside the settee where she could watch him, and
for the first time admitted the possibilty that
despite whatever she might say to herself to the
contrary, however she might try to rationalise her
feelings, and his, she was trapped. She was fighting
this battle, in other words, not to avenge herself,
but because she was falling deeper and deeper in
love with him—she was fighting for her life.

She moved restlessly, then looked at him
anxiously, but he didn't stir and she asked herself
how, why? The answers were plain enough. Why
else had she been like a cat on a hot tin roof this
past week, if it wasn't because she'd actually
missed him? Why else would she be so anxious not
to join the list of women he despised, and be able
to understand why it was that way for him, and be
able to hate his cynicism . . . but not him?

'Oh God,' she whispered, 'that's what's been
eluding me, I'm fighting this for real. Does he
know? Is *he* aware of this dangerous closeness that
I can't change, even if it's often bitter? Or is he still
playing me like a fish on a line?'

She closed her eyes on tears of confusion and
despair, then left very quietly.

Sunday was a tense uncomfortable day.

Away from him, she was uncertain again and
almost feverishly trying to persuade herself that she
could not have fallen in love with a man who didn't
believe in it.

Then, early in the afternoon, she suddenly
realised she had forgotten to get a present for

Pippa and Marcus, and she racked her brains for a solution to the problem, until she remembered Min's beautifully carved bookends. She dashed over to the office, praying no one else had nabbed them. But they were still there, and she left an IOU for them and rushed home with them thankfully.

But why am I *rushing* everything? she wondered, back in her apartment with the afternoon stretching emptily ahead of her. Everything about me is off key, out of tune, and I'm so afraid it's because . . .

But she wouldn't allow herself to think that thought. She *couldn't*. The prospect was too humiliating.

She started to get ready quite early, earlier than necessary—anything to pass the time. She was never quite sure what prompted her to wear what she did. At least, afterwards, she couldn't help wondering if she had surrendered to some subconscious urge, although at the time she'd only been determined to look her best.

She washed and blow-dried her hair, and for a change put it up on top of her head in a simple knot. It looked elegant, she decided, and made her look, if not older, more mature, somehow, more serious, although there was one disadvantage, it made her eyes look larger. And if your eyes are the window to your soul, she reflected rather grimly, that could be a serious disavantage. But she tightened her lips and left it up.

The next step was her underwear, and it was blatantly seductive—an all-in-one black lace garment that combined the functions of bra and suspender-belt with delicious, sensuous frivolity, that caressed her skin and caused it to gleam enticingly, and surprisingly had been a gift from her mother. In fact, Kirra had thought she'd got over being surprised by her mother, but this gift had proved her wrong. It was a crime not to wear this kind of thing while you'd still got the figure for it, her mother had said with a naughty little twinkle in her eye.

This was probably why it was hard for Kirra to associate the garment with any kind of sin, and anyway, she discovered she loved wearing the sheerest of stockings with it rather than tights.

The dress she put on was a deep shade of corn-flower-blue, figure-hugging with narrow shoulder straps, a tantalising little opening between her breasts, and a slash up the front from ankle to knee-line. It was a dress she'd worn before and not considered particularly daring.

She sat down to do her face, but even this procedure, done carefully and delicately, still left her with about forty-five minutes to kill. She looked around despairingly, but her bedroom was tidy, the rest of the apartment was tidied within an inch of its life, witness to a punishing bout of housekeeping yesterday, and there was nothing for her to do but sit and wait.

She shrugged and slipped on her grey kid shoes that were several shades darker than her stockings and wondered if she needed a drink to steady her nerves, but the thought annoyed her acutely.

So it was that all in all, by the time seven o'clock came around, she had worked herself into a state of simmering hostility and resentment.

'Come in,' she said carefully, opening the door to him. Her bare skimming glance took in his beautifully tailored grey suit, paler grey and white striped shirt, and blue tie. 'We have time for a drink, if you like.'

'No, thanks.' He followed her into the lounge. 'But . . .'

'Then I'll get my bag,' she said abruptly.

'Won't that make us early?' he asked idly, catching her hand as she went to sweep past him.

'Who cares?' she asked, staring at him tautly, hating him for his tall, cool composure when she felt the way she did.

'If that's the case,' he said abruptly, 'why are we bothering to go to this party at all?'

'Because it's better than sitting here, feeling trapped.' Her blue-grey eyes were defiant and her voice bitter.

'Trapped?' he questioned softly and with something like a glint of anger in his eyes. 'Or . . . wanting to do something else altogether? Such as this.' He released her hand and drew her into his arms.

Kirra shivered with a mixture of apprehension and anger, and he felt it and pulled her even closer with a mocking little smile. 'So fresh and perfumed and gorgeously groomed,' he marvelled. 'And as furious as a beautiful tigress wanting to be tamed, wanting it all to be undone, wanting to be stripped naked and thrown down on a bed, wanting to fight but be overpowered and . . . taken.'

'You . . .' she hissed, one hand unwittingly curling to claw his eyes out. 'That's disgusting!'

'Is it?' He released her and stared down at her sombrely. 'I think it's often the nature of things between men and women, whether we like it or not. Love is often savage and a lot of things we like to think it isn't.'

'You're talking about lust!'

'Call it what you like,' he said indifferently, 'just don't try to deny it exists between us by whatever name.'

'Right now, I'm prepared to deny it to the grave,' she said through her teeth. 'I . . . I'd rather consort with a . . . with a . . .'

'Snake?' he offered, barely audibly but with a glint in his hazel eyes that frightened her suddenly, made her catch her breath and wonder how he would retaliate, because she knew instinctively that he would.

She turned away jerkily.

But all he said, dispassionately she thought, was, 'Go and get your bag, then.'

She went with every nerve jangling and the heart-stopping, humiliating thought that he might have been right, that her feelings *had* descended to a savage desire for physical expression.

She stared at her bed and felt her cheeks begin to burn as the images he had triggered swept through her mind. 'No,' she whispered, appalled at what she was thinking, and she reached for her bag clumsily—and heard one of her sheer, beautiful grey stockings go ping.

She looked down and saw the ladder climbing to her knee. '*Damn!*' she muttered furiously.

She threw her bag back down on the bed and undid the stocking through the silky material of her dress. Then she hunted through a drawer, but the only grey ones she could find were a new pair and much lighter, which meant she would have to change both stockings. She kicked off her shoes and discarded the wrapping of cellophane and cardboard on to the floor, then started to peel the others off in a fever of irritation.

She never knew what alerted her, he'd made no sound on the thick carpeting, but just as she was standing on one foot with her dress hitched up around her hips, and just as she was securing the second of the new stockings on the leg poised on the end of the bed with her foot arched, she glanced up and he was there, standing in the doorway, watching her.

Her hands stilled and her heart started to beat erratically at the way he was watching her, and she followed his gaze to where her hands rested, to where the gauzy grey stocking gave way to the ivory, satin-smooth skin of her inner thigh.

Her lashes lifted and she looked over at him again, to see that curiously heavy-lidded gaze move up her. She glanced down, to see that because of the way she was standing with one shoulder slightly forward, the creamy and black-lace-shadowed curve of one breast was exposed where the opening at the front of her dress had fallen forward.

She looked up again and their gazes caught and held; she felt oddly naked but hypnotised beneath that all-encompassing hazel gaze. Then she forced herself to break the moment. She closed the last suspender unhurriedly and stood upright, smoothing the cornflower-blue silk as it slid down her body. Finally, she raised her chin and stared at him coolly.

But as he moved and strolled across the carpet towards her, she began to regret her hauteur and recall the instinctive feeling she'd had that he wouldn't allow her last insult to pass unavenged. She was not proved wrong.

He stopped right in front of her so that she had

to tilt her head back to look up at him.

'When we're married,' he drawled and raised a
hand to trail his fingers very lightly down the valley
between her breasts, then smooth the material
closed, 'you'll need some new clothes.'

Surprise made Kirra blink, which he observed
with his lips twisting into a cool smile, although his
eyes were not smiling. 'Yes,' he added thoughtfully. 'Because I don't think I'll enjoy other men
seeing your breasts and . . . lusting after you, from
my own point of view, but also from yours—you
who have such an inbuilt dislike of it, or so you tell
me.'

Sheer shock held Kirra rigid, her lips parted, her
eyes darkening, but that only brought another cool
smile to his lips and a glint of mockery to his eyes.
Then he said casually, 'Shall we go?'

'Darling!' Pippa breathed into Kirra's ear some
time after they had arrived. 'Why didn't you tell
me?'

Kirra stiffened and said warily, 'Tell you what?'

'Why you were so interested in Matthew
Remington!'

'Oh, that,' Kirra said lamely.

'Yes, that,' Pippa said ruefully. 'Do I detect an
air of mystery in your manner?'

'Not . . .' Kirra broke off and bit her lip.

Pippa narrowed her eyes thoughtfully. 'He is . . .
well, he almost defies description, doesn't he?'

He does that all right, Kirra thought bitterly.

'Or to put it right, Kirra thought bitterly.
one stumbles through this jungle of life, one
observes from time to time a king of the jungle, a
man among men for whom you'd gladly sell your

soul, despite the fact that you love your cuddly little husband.'

Despite *her* state of mind and the unfortunate allusion to jungles, Kirra couldn't help smiling, not only at Pippa's extravagant imagery, but because while Pippa was lean and elegant, Marcus was short as well as short-sighted, alternately earnest and playful, and bore no resemblance to the tiger king. But her smile was short-lived.

Pippa watched her expression change and she said slowly, 'Perhaps not an easy man to know, though. Want to tell me how things . . . stand between you?'

'Oh, Pip,' Kirra said, suddenly unable to hide the distress in her eyes, 'I wish I *knew*.'

Pippa looked concerned, then pressed Kirra's hand. 'If ever you do need a good listener, I'm always willing,' she said gently. 'Why don't you just relax and enjoy yourself for now?'

It was a successful party.

The new house was a dream, but then with Marcus and Pippa's combined talents it would have been surprising had it not been.

What surprised and amused a lot of people, although not Kirra, was their hosts' touching pride in it all—everyone got a complete guided tour of even the bathrooms, linen cupboard and laundry.

What did surprise Kirra was how many people seemed to know Matt, mostly men, admittedly, but their wives or girlfriends were obviously flattered and impressed to be introduced.

They ate caviare and lobster, drank champagne and danced on the red-flagged terrace beneath the stars—some even went for a swim in the floodlit pool.

Kirra visited one of Marcus's pride-and-joy bathrooms and, coming back, lingered for a moment just inside the lounge, where she could see Matt dancing with a languorous blonde, without being seen. And, as she watched, she saw him say something that made her laugh with no trace of languor.

Is that *expertise,* or just because he's *nice?* Kirra thought with a stab of resentment. He's certainly not making her feel like a tramp. I bet he would only have to snap his fingers and she'd leap . . . Oh hell, Kirra, you're not jealous, surely?

After midnight the party got livelier and noisier, but Kirra merely got more tired. It was an unbelievable strain dancing with Matt—it was a strain dancing with anyone, because she kept wondering how the front of her dress was behaving and kept getting angry with herself for bothering. Will this night never end? she asked herself wearily.

He chose to end it, for them at least, at about one-thirty. He said, 'You look as if you've had enough.'

She nodded, keeping her eyes veiled. And for the first time that evening he displayed some possessiveness. He took her hand and kept it in his while they made their farewells. And he held it as they walked down the driveway to the car, then he raised an eyebrow at her. 'Up or down?' He indicated the hood.

'Oh, down, I think,' she said. 'It's a beautiful night.'

She didn't protest when it became obvious they were not going straight home. Nor did she say anything when he parked the car beside a moonlit stretch of beach. She sat for a time watching and listening to the surf, then she put her hands up to her hair which was windblown and coming adrift, and eased the pins out and with a sigh of relief ran her fingers through it and laid her head back.

He turned to her and propped one arm along the back of the seat. 'You've been very quiet tonight, Kirra.'

'Sometimes champagne has that effect on me. Dulls the edges.' Something has dulled the rage anyway, she reflected. Was it the thought that it could have been the reverse side of a compelling desire to . . . submit?

'So it has nothing to do with what I said to you before the party?'

She turned her face to him without lifting her head. 'Of course it has,' she said with no anger, just sounding drained and weary.

'I'm sorry.'

'Are you?' she whispered after an age, staring at him, at the way the moonlight glinted on his fair hair, the lines of his face, the way he was tracing the spokes of the steering-wheel and watching what he was doing so that she couldn't read his eyes.

'Doesn't that help?' he said, looking up at last.

'It doesn't help the way I feel about myself.' She said it slowly and quietly, and a spark of irony flickered in her blue-grey eyes, then they focused on him again, her lashes forming perfect dark crescents, her face pale and curiously young looking.

'Are we getting closer to naming the day?'

Why did I ask that? she wondered immediately, and as soon as he spoke, knew.

He said drily, 'I'll consult my diary.'

She closed her eyes and thought, I was hoping you'd be honest with me and end this farce right now—that's why I asked that. Why don't I end it? What am I hoping for—a miracle?

She sat up abruptly. 'Could you take me home now?'

'Kirra . . .'

'*Please*—I'm tired.' Her voice was hoarse with sudden urgency.

He captured her chin and forced her to look at him, but some lingering spark of defiance made her lower her lashes and clamp her lips together until he smiled as drily as he'd spoken earlier, and released her to start the car up.

The drive home was swift and silent, so silent that she thought she could hear the clock ticking.

He didn't get out, he didn't even switch the engine off in the forecourt of her building. And all he said was, 'I'll be in touch.'

Kirra slipped out of the car and ran inside without a backward glance.

CHAPTER TEN

MIN surprised her the following morning by arriving unexpectedly.

She popped her head around Kirra's office door and said gaily, 'They're finished, done, and I hope to God you like them, otherwise I'll take them out and drown them!'

'Min! Glory be, that was quick work! Come in, it's great to see you. And I'm sure you won't have to drown them—how do you drown dolphins, anyway?'

Min chuckled. 'I'd have found a way. I brought one panel in to show you,' she had a heavy-looking parcel under her arm, 'and the rest are in the car.'

Min's dolphin panels were a great hit, and she secured two more commissions on the spot.

'Come and have lunch with me,' Kirra said impulsively.

'It should be my shout after . . .'

'Nonsense! You did all the work the last time we met—it's definitely mine!'

They chatted idly for a while over lunch, then Min said, 'How's Matt?'

'Fine. You haven't seen him since . . .?'

'No. It goes like that. Sometimes I don't see him for months. Are you . . . is he . . . are you two still together?' Min asked awkwardly.

Kirra studied her quiche rather attentively, then she sighed and said, 'As together as we're ever likely to be.'

'Would you like to tell me about it?' said Min gently.

'I . . .' Kirra hesitated.

'There would be no question of me ever repeating anything to Matt. He may be my friend, but you and I . . . well, I regard you as a friend, too.'

Kirra smiled at her and said quietly, 'Thanks. Well . . .' And to her surprise, she found herself telling Min everything. '. . . and when I discovered the contracts *were* signed, that he'd only been toying with me, I was . . . I was——' She broke off and grimaced. 'There's an old saying about hell having no fury like a woman scorned—I can vouch for it.'

'Because you'd fallen in love with him?' Min queried.

'That condition is something I've only fairly recently admitted to.' Kirra pushed her plate away. 'It was relatively easy to pretend otherwise while I thought he was forcing me to marry him. But much as I'd still like to think I hate him, I . . . I . . . it's as if my whole being is *centred* on him. It's very hard to explain,' she said helplessly. 'It's just as if he's the focus of my existence. When he's not around I can't settle to anything, when he is I alternate between . . . wanting him desperately and feeling as if I could kill him—anything.'

She winced and looked away, but when she looked back Min was only looking extremely thoughtful.

'Sorry,' said Kirra shakily. 'I didn't mean to sound so dramatic, nor do I always feel quite so violent about it. But I think,' she said slowly, 'there's only one thing I can do now, and that's put as much distance between us as I can.'

'There's something I don't understand, though,' Min said. 'If it's as you say, he's gone to extraordinary lengths either to teach you a lesson or to avenge his masculine pride, don't you think?'

Kirra shrugged. 'Perhaps he thought—well, here's one witless bird I *can* teach a lesson.'

'Do you honestly believe that?' Min asked softly.

'If I knew what to believe, I might not be in this mess. I can't help but believe women don't stand very high in his esteem.'

'That's true—*certain* kinds of women, and probably for all the usual reasons that good-looking, wealthy men are rather wary. But I happen to be . . . living proof, if you like, that he doesn't despise all women. You know,' Min paused, and there was suddenly a far-away look in her eyes, 'I sometimes wondered if it wasn't himself he despised.'

Kirra stared at her with her lips parted.

'For,' Min paused again, 'inheriting his father's fatal attraction for women. Perhaps, despite himself, *that's* the root of some of his cynicism.'

'I . . . oh!' Kirra said, barely audibly.

'Yes,' Min agreed.

Kirra was silent, then she said, almost to herself, 'He is . . . the only time or one of the very few times I've got beneath his skin has been in relation to his father. I mean, he told me quite readily he didn't like him and why, but . . . once, anyway, I thought there might be more to it, although I couldn't put my finger on it. On the other hand,' she said with a frown, 'he hasn't exactly gone out of his way to . . . do things differently from his father, has he?'

'Hasn't he?' Min murmured. 'He's committed himself to no one—sure, he's played the field and probably often with the sort of indifference that's tantamount to a calculated insult. Perhaps it's even been a test,' Min moved her hands, 'a sort of standing back and saying, if all it takes is a bit of physical expertise . . .' She grimaced, then went on, 'I can't believe it was indifference that prompted him to do this to you, though, Kirra. I think you must have hit a nerve.'

Kirra put a hand to her mouth. 'If I thought understanding would help . . . And I do understand, but how to get across that I do?'

'Maybe you can only love him,' Min said wisely.

Kirra thought about what Min had said all that afternoon, and that evening she stayed at home in case Matt rang, but he didn't.

Instead, he took her to lunch the next day. He simply turned up at her office doorway much as Min had done the day before, and the unexpectedness of looking up and seeing him caught her off guard, so that a tide of pink rose up in her cheeks, her pulses started to hammer and she got up jerkily, knocking over a glazed pottery urn standing on her desk.

It was he who strode forward to catch it before it hit the floor.

'Oh . . . thank God,' she breathed.

'Valuable?' he asked.

'Very, and very old. I don't know how I came to be so clumsy.'

He said gravely, 'I didn't mean to startle you so.'

'You didn't,' she said, then coloured because that was patently untrue.

But he didn't comment, and he put the urn down carefully and ran his hands over it. Then he stepped back and studied her thoughtfully, until she smoothed her buttercup linen dress uncomfortably and said foolishly, 'Did you want to see me about something?'

A faint smile twisted his lips. 'I just wanted to see

you. Can I buy you lunch?'

She stared at him and felt her stomach churn with the knowledge that here was the opportunity to do what she knew she had to—if she was brave enough.

'Thanks,' she said quietly. 'It so happens I've got the afternoon off.'

He took her to Nicolini's at Mariner's Cove, and they sat outside on the veranda beneath the awning, with the Broadwater stretching away from them, dancing in the sunlight and studded with millions of dollars'-worth of boats at their moorings.

They both chose prawns Nicolini and a salad—and Kirra could think of nothing to say, no way to begin . . .

Nor did he make any move to push the conversation until they were half finished, when he said idly, watching her as her gaze rested on a sleek, gleaming, fly-bridge cruiser, 'Would you like a boat for a wedding present?'

Kirra averted her gaze hastily. 'No, thank you.'

'That's a pity—we could have called it the *Lady Kirralee*,' he drawled. 'What would you like? You could have almost anything in reason, you know.'

'Is that . . .' her voice quivered, 'why you asked me to lunch? To insult me?' Their eyes clashed, and hers were more blue than grey, like the water beside them, and suddenly very steady as she added, 'To continue to insult me, I should have said.'

He raised an eyebrow. 'I gather this is where we . . . deal in the truth. What, as a matter of interest, decided you to show your hand at last?'

'You knew I knew?' she queried incredulously.

'I guessed,' he murmured. 'You had to find out sooner or later.'

'Your . . . sheer cold-bloodedness is almost

unbelievable,' Kirra said with an effort.

'Is it?' he said softly. 'The offer is still open, by the way. Will you marry me, Kirra?'

'If this is another . . .'

'It's not. Will you?'

She searched his eyes dazedly. 'I don't understand.'

'That I want to marry you?'

'No—no, I don't.'

'You don't agree that we're rather well matched?' he said, and his hazel eyes were suddenly compelling.

'Have I . . . have I passed some sort of test I wasn't even aware of?' she asked huskily.

'Perhaps,' he said very quietly, and now his eyes were hooded, she thought, unreadable and sombre, and beneath the smooth, thick fair hair the lines of his face were harsh. And just to look at him hurt her, not only because she loved him and could never deny it to herself again, but also because she knew him now as she thought she would never know another man or want to—but knew she couldn't change him.

'Tell me something, Matt.' She fiddled with the salt-cellar, turning it round and round in her slim, beautifully manicured fingers. Then she put it down and lifted her eyes to his. 'Why did you . . . issue that ultimatum under such false pretences?'

He sat back in his chair. 'I did it on the spur of the moment. You were so haughty—and so beautiful.' Their gazes locked and held. 'I thought it could be a way to find out what really made you tick, Kirra.'

'And now you have . . . at least, you've found out I won't go to bed with you. Was that the test I passed?'

He was silent, but she saw the ironic little salute in his eyes, and closed her own briefly.

'That . . . disturbs you?' he asked.

Kirra stared down at her hands, and at the two delicious prawns on her plate she knew she could not eat. 'Yes. Yes, it does,' she whispered.

'It seemed to be very important to *you,*' he said drily.

'It was—but all the same we were at cross purposes. And we still are. I don't believe your . . . test was conclusive of anything other than a deeply rooted cynical indifference . . . which, I grant you, you've never tried to deny. But I couldn't live with that. That's why it was so important to *me.*'

'On the other hand, Kirra, don't you think we've forged a kind of unity throughout this . . . contest, if you like? We want each other and no one else. We . . . we can even read each other's minds,' he said with a grim little smile, and when her eyes flew to his, he went on, 'I knew that night I phoned you from Melbourne that you'd found out the contracts had been signed. You knew, if you're prepared to admit it, from not much later that I was only humouring you.'

Did I? she wondered with an inward tremor. 'Humouring me?' she repeated, however, and her eyes were bitter.

'Don't tell me you didn't know that the game was no longer a game,' he said roughly.

She coloured, but said steadily, 'I could be forgiven for thinking it was always a game to you.'

His gaze was sardonic.

'All right,' she said quietly. 'Although I didn't admit it to myself, I think I must have . . . I did know it wasn't a game. Not for me, at least,' she said barely audibly.

'Or for me,' he insisted.

'All the same,' and her voice was unsteady now, 'I can't marry you, Matt. Foolishly or otherwise, I want more than you can give.'

'You still don't know what I *can* give you, Kirra,' he said harshly.

'Yes, I do,' she whispered. 'A marriage composed of tests—I'm bound to fail one sooner or later.' She dashed at the tears on her lashes. 'I've done some stupid things since I met you, Matt, but as I mentioned once before, I've also learnt a lot. The answer is no, and nothing you can say will make me change my mind. I . . . I think I'd better go now.'

He stood up and dropped some money on to the table.

'I can get a taxi home,' she said shakily, but he put out a hand to help her up. Nor did he let go of her arm until they were at the car. But he said nothing on the short drive to Main Beach.

Then he switched the engine off and turned to her. 'If it's a declaration of undying, eternal love you want, Kirra, I have to tell you the words alone mean nothing, and if someone else ever says them to you, just remember this, I never swore anything to you or made you any false promises, but I think I know you better than any other man ever will.'

Her breath came in a surprised little jolt as his words echoed her earlier thoughts.

'And to me, that's what it's all about. I'm sorry . . . we differ there.'

He put out a hand and touched her hair, then his lips twisted as she looked away, then back at him, and said simply, 'So am I. Goodbye, Matt.'

'Goodbye, Kirra.'

Hours later, she sat in her apartment, dry-eyed but

feeling incredibly bereft, and in her agony she'd been over everything he had ever said and done to her and all her reactions and responses, as if searching for a truth that still eluded her. The conviction, for example, they each held that they understood one another better than anyone else would—should that be enough to base a lifetime commitment on, as he had suggested? Did her conviction that it wasn't stem from an over-emotional, sentimental view of love?

'Whatever,' she whispered at last, hugging a cushion to herself, 'I made the decision . . . because I can't change myself.' And the tears came at last, but they didn't heal the feeling of loss, and she wondered if anything ever would.

CHAPTER ELEVEN

THREE months later Kirra got home from work and withdrew a slim folder from her bag, then sat down to study the contents—brochures, stickers and an airline ticket, destinations Hong Kong and Singapore.

Her date of departure was a fortnight away.

She studied them for a few minutes, then with a sigh put them away, because she knew this trip was not going to excite her, it was more in the nature of a desperate attempt to forget.

She had seen and heard nothing from Matt, although she'd heard of him through her parents and been on the receiving end of their delicate probings as to why such a promising beginning had apparently died such a swift death. These she'd parried as well as she was able to, and she had also gone out of her way to hide from them the fact that she had lost some weight and was still, three months on, not sleeping well. She'd done this by being as active as possible socially, but there were times when her mother looked at her assessingly and seemed set to say something, but changed her mind at the last minute.

It had been on the last of those occasions that Kirra had decided she had to get away.

'Well, now I'm going,' she said to herself, getting up to draw the curtains on a cool, autumn evening. 'I've always wanted to see Hong Kong and Singapore —surely I can dredge up some enthusiasm?'

*   *   *

The foyer of the Mandarin Hotel, Hong Kong, was a symphony of gold and black, and Kirra was immediately impressed by the air of elegance, and more particularly by the absence of flurry which had formed her first impressions of Hong Kong since her Cathay Pacific flight had landed a few hours ago. In fact, it would be accurate to say that the traffic had been mind-boggling, and she had gazed out of the window of the car that had transported her from Kai Tak airport to the hotel, via the Harbour Tunnel from Kowloon to Hong Kong Island, with wide eyes. Not only the traffic but the people, and even now she stared over her shoulder out through the main doors to the chaos of Connaught Road, and wondered if she would ever be game to leave the sanctuary of the Mandarin.

But perhaps that's exactly what I need, she mused, a challenge—something to get me functioning properly again. After a good long sleep, though, she added to herself. I feel as if I've been on that plane for nineteen hours instead of nine . . .

'Miss Munro?'

She turned from the reception desk where she was registering with a little start of surprise. 'Yes?'

'Miss Munro, may I introduce myself? I'm the manager, and I've had the pleasure of welcoming Sir Kenneth and Lady Munro to the Mandarin several times.'

'Oh,' Kirra smiled, 'I know. They were quite adamant I should stay here and nowhere else. How do you do?'

'Miss Munro . . .' The man in the pin-striped black suit hesitated, and Kirra's smiled faded after a moment.

'Is something wrong?'

'I'm so sorry to have to be the bearer of these tidings, but your mother has been taken ill, Miss Munro.'

'Ill,' Kirra said dazedly. 'Seriously?'

'Rather seriously, but please, would you come into my office? We can . . .'

'But I've got to get home! Right now . . . oh, please,' she said desperately. 'I . . .'

'That's what I hope to be able to arrange for you. Please come this way, Miss Munro.'

If her first flight had felt prolonged, the one she caught home after a stay of only eight hours in Hong Kong—all of them wide awake—seemed never-ending. She couldn't sleep, she barely ate, and for the first time in her life suffered acute claustrophobia on a plane. And she couldn't concentrate on anything other then the vision of her mother, the victim of a stroke and in intensive care.

Fortunately, she flew direct to Brisbane instead of via Sydney as the flight to Hong Kong had taken her. And when she landed, feeling terrible and no doubt looking it, the prospect of the long trudge through Customs and Immigration made her feel like screaming. But someone must have alerted the authorities, because she was processed first, and, although she was very grateful, she couldn't help wondering if it was an ominous sign.

The last person she expected to meet her beyond the swinging doors and the barrier was Matt; Matt in a dark suit and a white shirt, his face unreadable.

'Have . . . have you come to meet me?' she stammered.

'Yes.'

'Oh, how is she?' she whispered, her control

breaking at last and tears streaming down her face. 'Is . . .' She realised to her embarrassment that she was clutching the front of his jacket.

'She's holding her own, Kirra,' he said quietly, scanning her pale face with a frown in his eyes, and he put an arm round her. 'Come.'

She hid her face in his shoulder for a moment, then took a grip on herself. 'How are you?'

'Fine,' he said briefly, and for an instant, as they stared at each other, everything that had fascinated and tormented her about him rose up in her heart in a living tide of despair. He looked exactly the same and she remembered suddenly how, right from the beginning, she'd rejoiced in his looks, although her vision of him had been false. Or was it? she wondered. Even then you knew he was a loner at heart.

She tore her gaze away and bent to pick up her bags, which were absurdly light, but he took them from her and remarked on the fact.

She grimaced. 'They say you should go to Hong Kong in only what you stand up in, because things are so cheap there—I took them at their word.'

He smiled faintly, and led the way to the car.

It was a swift trip to the coast, and Kirra's desperate concern for her mother had swept all other emotions away again.

Matt told her all he knew of her mother's condition, and half-way there he pulled out a silver flask and handed it to her. 'Brandy,' he said, his eyes flickering over her. 'Have some. Have you eaten lately?'

'I couldn't.'

'You must eat,' he said gently. 'It will help no one if you collapse.' And he pulled into a road-house and bought her a toasted chicken sandwich and a chocolate bar. To her surprise, she ate both and then had another sip of the neat brandy.

'Thanks,' she murmured. 'I do feel a bit stronger now.'

He took a hand from the wheel and put it over hers.

That night was the longest night of Kirra's life, as she and her father comforted each other and kept a vigil over her mother.

'I don't know what I'd do without her,' her father kept saying. 'She means more to me than anything.'

'I know, I know,' Kirra kept answering, wincing at his anguish added to her own.

But the early hours of the morning brought good news.

'She's been very lucky, Sir Kenneth,' the doctor told them. 'There may be some slight paralysis, but she's definitely out of danger now, I'm happy to be able to tell you.'

Kirra clung to her father, weeping tears of joy, as was he, and Matt, who had not intruded on their vigil but kept them supplied with coffee, sighed with obvious relief.

Then Matt and her father spoke together quietly for a while, and her father came over to her and said, 'My dear, Matt is going to take you home.'

'But . . .'

'Darling, you must be exhausted.'

'So are you!'

He smiled tiredly. 'I haven't flown half-way across the world and back in the last two days, but they're going to fix me up a bed here. Go home and have a sleep, so that when she's more lucid, you'll be fresh and rested.'

It was raining outside and she nearly fell asleep in the car, but when they got upstairs to her apartment she felt wide awake again.

'Thanks,' she said awkwardly as he unlocked the door for her. 'You don't have to . . . stay.'

'Yes, I do,' he replied with a critical look at her, and he followed her in and closed the door. 'Why don't you have a bath? I'll make some breakfast.'

'Well, but you must be tired too, and I haven't got anything to make for breakfast.'

'Kirra,' he said with a wry look, 'don't argue. Just do as you're told. I'll go and get something to make for breakfast.'

The bath was heavenly, more so because it was a chilly grey morning and the rain was teeming down now. And as she lay in the steaming, scented water she felt her nerves beginning to unwind. She also sniffed appreciatively as the aroma of grilled bacon filtered into the bathroom.

They ate the bacon and eggs in a queer sort of harmony, as if they were curiously insulated from all that had happened between them.

She told him about her confused impressions of Hong Kong, and he told her it had taken him two trips before he had got the hang of the place. He mentioned that Min had decided she was brave enough to come out of seclusion, and Kirra said warmly that she was happy for Min. Then she asked him what he would do about the horses and the house, and he said he would board the horses out on a neighbouring property and shut up the house.

All so natural, one small portion of Kirra's tired brain marvelled, but in no way could she come to grips with this phenomenon.

He made them coffee and she closed her eyes and drank it slowly.

'To bed now, I think,' he said quietly.

'Yes,' she murmured, finding it hard to keep her eyes open.

'Off you go—I'll clean up.'

She stood up and stared down at him for a long moment, not knowing what to say, and in the end said only, 'Thanks.'

He didn't reply, but he looked away first.

She fell asleep almost immediately—only to wake in minutes, with her heart pounding, her mouth dry and her nerves tightened to screaming-point. And when she managed to calm herself a little, it occurred to her that she wasn't going to be able to sleep—that she should not have rejected the mild sedative the doctor had offered her, that she was dangerously over-tired and over-wrought.

That was how Matt found her, sitting up with her head in her hands, and it was the quiet opening of the door that made her look up.

'What is it?' he asked, coming over to the bed.

'I can't sleep,' she whispered helplessly. 'I'm . . . a nervous wreck.' She tried to smile, but it didn't come off; and then she was crying, silently.

He sat down and took her in his arms and stroked her hair. 'Yes, you can,' he murmured. 'I'll help you.'

'I feel such a fool,' she wept.

'Why? You're only over-tired.'

'I know that, but . . .'

He released her and brushed some wet strands of hair off her face. 'Lie down,' he said.

'W-where are you going?' she stammered, sliding

down.

'Nowhere,' he said, lying down beside her and adjusting the covers so that, although he was on top of them, he could put his arms around her. 'I'm tired too. We might as well be tired together. You smell like a rose.'

'That's my bath oil,' she said dazedly.

'Comfortable?'

'Mmm . . .'

'Close your eyes, then.'

'I . . . I'm afraid to.'

'No, you're not. Think of something nice. Roses, seeing as you smell like one. Slim little salmon-pink buds wrapped in cellophane, or—lovely blowsy full-blown cream ones with bees buzzing around them, mysterious dark velvety red ones . . .'

Kirra never knew afterwards whether it was the roses he brought to mind so vividly, or the safe strong feel of his arms, his breath on her cheek, his quiet, deep voice that mesmerised her into slipping unknowingly into sleep, a deep, dreamless sleep for hours.

When she woke, the rain had stopped and the sun was shining, it was well after mid-day, and she was alone.

Or so she thought when she reached unthinkingly across the bed before she was properly awake, then sat up, pushing her hair back and looking around, still drowsy and disorientated.

He was standing in the doorway, leaning against the frame with his jacket hooked over his shoulder, his tie undone and his hair lying across his forehead.

She said his name uncertainly, and he straightened and started to speak, but she interrupted him.

'Don't go, please,' she whispered.

'I must,' he said, his hazel gaze sombre as it swept over her briefly, her hair, her bare shoulders beneath the narrow shoulder straps of her grey silk night-gown, the outline of her breasts, then back to her eyes. 'If I stay,' he said, barely audibly, and with a nerve flickering in his jaw, 'I might do something we . . . could regret.'

'No,' she said equally quietly. 'There could be no regrets. I . . . need you, Matt. Please stay . . .'

CHAPTER TWELVE

'HOLD it!' the photographer said enthusiastically. Then, 'Excellent. Now if I could just take one last one of Mrs Remington and the baby.'

It was a small christening party, comprising Kirra's parents, Pippa and Marcus, Min and her escort—a big, quiet-spoken man who was obviously in love with her, and Stanley, who had made the cake and insisted on acting as butler and chief nurser of André Remington, who, at just three months, had slept through the proceedings so far.

But although small in numbers it had been a lively gathering at the house on the hill overlooking the Tweed River, and Kirra glanced around with deep affection as she accepted André from his maternal grandmother, whose only visible after-effect of the stroke she'd suffered was a slight limp.

She didn't notice Stanley charging everyone's glasses as she sat for the last photo; in fact, she'd transferred her gaze to her sleeping son, who was so like his father that it still amazed her. And her thoughts were on the fact that he was due for a feed and would soon wake and indicate this to her with a determination that was also reminiscent of his father. Nor did she look up immediately when the camera flashed, and for a moment no one said a word, as they all watched her sitting there in her wistaria-blue dress with a small white voile collar and cuffs, her hair loose and lying on her shoulders, and her obvious preoccupation with her son.

Then Sir Kenneth cleared his throat and proposed a simple toast. 'To Kirra,' he said, raising his glass.

She looked up at last, taken unawares, and went faintly pink as almost everyone echoed her father's words, and she looked directly at Matt, the only one who had not participated, but as their eyes met he raised his glass in a silent, lingering salute, and she saw in their hazel depths a look she was now very familiar with. A look that told her he would with great diplomacy end the party soon, and after she had fed his son he would make love to her in a way that even after nearly two years of marriage made her tremble to think of it.

The sun had slipped behind Mount Warning and Murwillumbah, and its fiery splendour was fading when Kirra prepared to go downstairs, having bathed and fed André and put him to bed.

She had changed into an ivory and red silk caftan with a tissuey gold border on the wide sleeves and hem that brushed the floor. Matt had bought it for her in Hong Kong, where they had spent part of their honeymoon, after a wedding which had taken place only a few days after she had returned from her first, abortive trip there. But she lingered a while, fingering the gold tissue on her sleeve and staring out over the darkening landscape, thinking about their marriage and how it had taken place by mutual, almost unspoken consent, as if it had been inevitable—the unalterable consequence of their physical union. And thinking that what was between them was still unspoken. Apart from their marriage vows, they had made no undying declarations to each other, but somehow he had bound her to him more closely each succeeding day. She sometimes wondered if he would

ever say the words she had longed to hear, she
sometimes longed to say them herself, but never did.
Instead she accepted his passion and matched it, as
she had accepted his care and compassion through a
rather arduous first pregnancy and birth, and she had
told herself she didn't need the words, she was
content and at peace, she would never press him—it
was the nature of things between them . . .

He was waiting for her in the lounge with a tray of
smoked-salmon sandwiches set on the low table
before the stone fireplace, and two glasses of wine
poured, and he had changed too, into jeans and a
navy blue sports shirt. His fair hair was damp and
awry, and his feet were bare as he lounged on the
leather settee.

'Settled?' he asked with a lift of an eyebrow.

'Yes.' She smiled faintly. 'I don't think being
christened made any impression on him at all.'

'He's a young man with rather a one-track mind,
I've noticed,' Matt said with a grin. 'The curious
thing is that we share . . . that track.'

'*I've* noticed that,' Kirra murmured. 'Must be
what that old saying—like father like son—is all
about.'

He reached for her hand and pulled her down
beside him. 'How does it feel to have,' he paused,
and his voice was curiously husky as he went on, 'the
absolute devotion of two males with one-track
minds?'

Kirra went still, and when she turned her head to
look at him, her blue-grey eyes were wary and
startled. 'You don't,' she cleared her throat, 'you
don't have to say that.'

'Don't I?' He bent his head and fiddled with her

gold wedding band, the only ring he'd ever given her. 'Personally I think it's long overdue,' he went on, and raised his eyes at last.

'Matt,' she whispered and realised she was shaking, 'I . . .' But she couldn't go on for a time, and they could only stare at each other until she said, 'Why now? Is it . . . because of André? Or have I passed . . .'

She stopped as his grasp on her hand tightened almost unbearably, and he said with barely suppressed savagery, 'The only test applicable between us is the gauge of my insanity, my inability to understand that nothing is ever going to make me stop loving you. You once said to me something about joy . . . watching you this afternoon filled me with pride and joy and something else, the knowledge that I could never let you go.' His lips twisted wryly. 'So from being a disbeliever,' he said with obvious self-directed mockery, 'I've become . . . perhaps the worst kind of believer: possessive, obsessed, all those things I swore never to be. Do you think you'll mind?'

'Oh God,' Kirra said hoarsely, her throat working and tears starting in her eyes.

He swore beneath his breath and pulled her into his arms. 'I didn't mean to sound flippant,' he said roughly. 'I'm deadly serious. I love you, Kirra . . . and if it's been too long in coming, I'm sorry, so sorry. I saw you,' he said with an effort, 'after André was born, when you were exhausted and hurting, look at me for an instant as if you were searching for something, and when you didn't see it, you closed your eyes briefly, but then you looked at me again and smiled . . . That's when I knew it had happened. That I loved you not only because you were beautiful and proud, but strong and committed and faithful.'

'Why . . .'

'Why didn't I say so then?' He sighed. 'If the truth be told, I've never known how to put into words how I felt about you. And even then—even now—it's much deeper than the words can say it. I . . . asked you to marry me several times in several ways, and when we did, we didn't say much at all. Would you think I was crazy if I said this time was for real?'

She stared at him with her lips parted, until he grimaced and he murmured, 'No, my darling Kirra, I haven't gone round the bend, but along with everything else I've become, all those things I mentioned, I've also discovered a streak of pure sentimentality. Which was why I thought this might be a fitting occasion to,' he reached down between the cushions and withdrew two grey velvet boxes, 'give you these.'

Her eyes widened.

'This one,' he said, handing her the smaller box, 'is an engagement ring. Open it.'

She pressed the catch and couldn't contain a gasp of delight at the ring nestled in the white satin lining. It wasn't large or ostentatious, and it wasn't the conventional diamond or sapphire. In fact, it was the most unusual and beautiful engagement ring she had seen: an amethyst in an antique gold setting and flanked by two small, milky opals that nevertheless gleamed green and gold and pink as they caught the light.

'It's exquisite,' she said huskily.

'Like it?'

'It's just beautiful. Thank you.' She blinked away some tears.

'I thought you might prefer it to a ball and chain,' he said with a wicked little glint in his eye, 'although I got one of those, too. As a memento.'

She looked at him and then down as he flicked open the second box and revealed another amethyst, a round one, a lovely pure violet-pink stone rimmed with gold and attached to a fine gold chain.

'Oh Matt,' she breathed, picking it up between her fingers.

'If I'm any judge,' he said, capturing her face in his hands, 'it will be a very private memento, this one . . . I'll show you what I mean in a moment, but can I put the ring on?'

She held out her left hand and he slid it on in front of her wedding band, then lifted his eyes to hers. 'Do you feel married to me now in every sense of the word, Kirra?' he queried.

She stared at him with all her love for him showing in her eyes at last. And she said, 'I do.' And raised her mouth for his kiss.

It was later when she stirred in his arms and remembered the amethyst ball and chain. 'You were going to show me something,' she said softly.

'Ah, yes.' He reached out a hand and switched on a lamp, and took it from her. 'Just one thing—you'd have to get undressed.'

'Why is that?' she asked innocently.

'That's the private nature of it.'

'I see. Well, perhaps you'd like to . . . do the honours.'

His eyes gleamed, but he said formally, 'Very well, Mrs Remington, if you insist.'

But he undressed her very slowly, stopping frequently to slide his lips and fingers along the smooth, glossy hollows and curves of her body that he now knew so well, and as always his touch was so light, she couldn't understand why it was like a trail of fire . . .

When he took her dress off, he eased her upright on the settee so that she was kneeling with her hands curved about his neck, and one by one he undid the long row of tiny buttons down the front, and when they were all undone she dropped her arms so that the material could slide off her shoulders with a soft, sibilant shush.

Their eyes caught and held, but he didn't immediately undo her bra. He cupped her shoulders in his palms instead and his long fingers slid beneath the straps, playing over her skin. He drew her close, and she tipped her head back so that he could kiss her throat, then lower and lower, until it became a sweet kind of torment that her breasts weren't free.

'Please,' she whispered, and he obliged, sliding his hands under her arms and releasing the catch and drawing it off her.

Then he took his hands away and she knelt with her ivory and gold dress clinging to her hips, her eyes solemn and a little questioning when his hands didn't come back to her.

But he had picked up the amethyst again, and with grave intent put it round her neck, fumbling a little with the catch, then, when it was done up, straightening the chain and the stone so that it hung between her breasts.

Kirra looked down at last, then up into his eyes.

'I thought,' he said softly, 'you might like to wear it only when we're going to make love.'

'I think that's a brilliant idea,' she whispered, her lips curving into a smile.

'Do you remember,' he said not quite evenly, playing with the amethyst, 'when you thought you might not be very good at . . . that?'

'Making love? Yes,' she said gravely.

'You were dead wrong, you know. I say that because I still want you beyond all belief.'

'Can I say what I think?'

'Please do,' he invited, moving his hands over her caressingly.

'I wasn't wrong. It's you. You've wrought the miracle. And it's because I love you and always will.'

'Kirra, darling,' his eyes were bright in the moment before he drew her into his arms and held her as if he would never let her go, 'that's my line.'

CHRISTMAS IS FOR KIDS

Spend this holiday season with nine very special children. Children whose wishes come true at the magical time of Christmas.

Read American Romance's CHRISTMAS IS FOR KIDS— heartwarming holiday stories in which children bring together four couples who fall in love. Meet:

Frank, Dorcas, Kathy, Candy and Nicky—They become friends at St. Christopher's orphanage, but they really want to be adopted and become part of a real family, in #321 *A Carol Christmas* by Muriel Jensen.

Patty—She's a ten-year-old certified genius, but she wants what every little girl wishes for: a daddy of her own, in #322 *Mrs. Scrooge* by Barbara Bretton.

Amy and Flash—Their mom is about to deliver their newest sibling any day, but Christmas just isn't the same now—not without their dad. More than anything they want their family reunited for Christmas, in #323 *Dear Santa* by Margaret St. George.

Spencer—Living with his dad and grandpa in an all-male household has its advantages, but Spence wants Santa to bring him a mommy to love, in #324 *The Best Gift of All* by Andrea Davidson.

These children will win your hearts as they entice—and matchmake—the adults into a true romance. This holiday, invite them—and the four couples they bring together—into your home.

Look for all four CHRISTMAS IS FOR KIDS books coming in December from Harlequin American Romance. And happy holidays!

You'll flip . . . your pages won't!
Read paperbacks *hands-free* with

Book Mate • I

The perfect "mate" for all your romance paperbacks

Traveling • Vacationing • At Work • In Bed • Studying • Cooking • Eating

Perfect size for all standard paperbacks, this wonderful invention makes reading a pure pleasure! Ingenious design holds paperback books OPEN and FLAT so even wind can't ruffle pages — leaves your hands free to do other things. Reinforced, wipe-clean vinyl-covered holder flexes to let you turn pages without undoing the strap . . . supports paperbacks so well, they have the strength of hardcovers!

Pages turn WITHOUT opening the strap

SEE-THROUGH STRAP

Reinforced back stays flat

Built in bookmark

BOOK MARK

BACK COVER HOLDING STRIP

10 x 7¼ opened
Snaps closed for easy carrying, too